Tales From Every Corner

"Exciting Stories
From All Over The Globe"

Syeda Saima Jawid

(a.ka. Seemie Jafri)

2025

Copyright

Published in 2025 by Green Zone Publishing
A division of Dr. Sohail MPC Inc.
213 Byron St. South
Whitby, Ontario Canada L1N 4P7
T. 905-666-7253   F. 905-666-4397
E-mail: welcome@drsohail.com
Website: www.drsohail.com

Syeda Saima Jawid
Tales From Every Corner
"Exciting Stories From All Over The Globe"

ISBN: 978-1-927874-69-1

Cover Design: Vicky Chen
Textual Design: Marcelina Naini

Table of Contents

The Silver Snow Fox and The Star

(A Story From Russia)

Long ago, in a far northern village where the snowflakes danced like feathers in the wind, there lived a young snow fox named *Anya*. Anya had fur as white as the winter snow and eyes that sparkled like the stars above. She was known for her cleverness and bravery, but more than anything, she had an insatiable curiosity. She loved listening to the elders' tales about the mystical Crystal Mountain, where a Silver Star lay hidden, and whoever found it would be granted incredible wisdom.

One frosty evening, Anya overheard a conversation between two old wolves. They spoke of the Silver Star and the great challenge one must face to find it. "Only those who can solve the riddles of the ancient forest will be allowed to approach the Crystal Mountain," one wolf said.

Anya's heart swelled with excitement. She was determined to find the Silver Star, not only for its wisdom but to prove that she was clever enough to solve the riddles and face whatever challenges lay ahead.

The next morning, after the sun had barely risen over the snowy horizon, Anya set out on her journey, her paws crunching softly in the fresh snow. As she journeyed deeper into the forest, the trees grew taller, their branches heavy with snow. Anya's path was guided by the shimmering glow of the northern lights overhead.

After hours of walking, Anya finally arrived at the foot of the Crystal Mountain. The peak sparkled in the sunlight, but at the base of the mountain, there stood a giant, glowing tree — a tree unlike any she had ever seen. The tree's bark shimmered with silver light, and its branches reached high into the sky. Beneath the tree sat a wise old owl named *Baba Yaga*.

Baba Yaga was known as the guardian of the Silver Star, and her riddles were said to be impossible to solve. With a deep hoot, Baba Yaga greeted Anya.

"You have come to claim the Silver Star, young fox. But first, you must answer my riddles," Baba Yaga said, her eyes glowing with ancient knowledge.

Anya nodded eagerly, her tail flicking with excitement. "I'm ready."

The owl spoke the first riddle:

"I have no voice, but I can speak to you. I have no body, but I can be touched. What am I?"

Anya sat in the snow, thinking hard. The cold air stung her nose, but she didn't mind. She had solved many puzzles in her life and knew she could figure this one out too.

"I know!" she exclaimed, her eyes bright. "It's a *thought*! A thought has no voice, but it can speak to you in your mind. And you can touch it by focusing on it."

Baba Yaga's eyes twinkled. "Well done, Anya. You have solved the first riddle. But there is still one more to face."

The owl's feathers ruffled as she spoke the second riddle:

"I can travel the world, but I stay in one place. I can be seen but never touched. I light the sky, but never burn. What am I?"

Anya felt the weight of the riddle on her mind. She gazed up at the sparkling lights of the aurora above. She knew she had seen the answer somewhere before, but where?

Then it came to her. "The *star*!" Anya said with a leap. "A star can be seen in the sky, but it never moves from its place. It lights the sky without burning."

Baba Yaga nodded approvingly. "You are indeed clever, Anya. You have answered both riddles. You are worthy of the Silver Star."

With a graceful flap of her wings, Baba Yaga gestured toward the Crystal Mountain. A gentle wind began to blow, and the top of the mountain shimmered with a silver light. Slowly, a shining star appeared at the peak, descending toward Anya. It was the Silver Star, glowing brightly with ancient wisdom.

As Anya touched the Silver Star, a warm feeling spread through her body, filling her with knowledge and understanding. She could hear the whispers of the winds, the stories of the earth, and the songs of the sky. The wisdom of the ages flowed into her, and she understood the importance of balance in the world, the harmony between the cold and the warmth, the day and the night.

Baba Yaga spoke again, her voice gentle. "The Silver Star has granted you wisdom, but remember, young fox, that true wisdom lies not in keeping knowledge to yourself, but in sharing it with others."

Anya nodded thoughtfully, her heart full of gratitude. She knew that her journey was not over. With the wisdom she had gained, she would help her fellow creatures in the forest, guiding them through hardships and teaching them the balance of nature.

As she returned to her village, Anya shared the lessons she had learned with the animals of the forest. The once-chilly winds became softer, and the snowflakes seemed to dance in a more harmonious rhythm. The animals, now wiser and more understanding, lived in peaceful unity, knowing that wisdom was not just for one, but for all.

And so, Anya the Snow Fox became a legend, not just for her cleverness, but for her kindness, sharing the wisdom of the Silver Star with everyone she met.

Moral of The Story

True wisdom is not something to be hoarded but shared. The more you share what you know, the more the world around you grows in harmony and understanding.

Riddles *

- ❖ *"I have no voice, but I can speak to you. I have no body, but I can be touched. What am I?"*
- ❖ *"I can travel the world, but I stay in one place. I can be seen but never touched. I light the sky, but never burn. What am I?"*

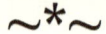

The Wise Sparrow
and The Golden Pomegranate
(A Story From Iran)

Long long ago, in a small village in northern Iran, there lived a curious and clever sparrow named *Kian*. His feathers were a mix of rich browns and golden hues, matching the warm tones of the landscape. Kian was known throughout the village not only for his intelligence but for his kind heart. He would often visit the villagers, listening to their stories and offering helpful advice.

One warm spring morning, as Kian perched on a tree, he overheard two elders talking about a hidden treasure deep within the mountains. The treasure, they said, was the legendary Golden Pomegranate—fruit that was said to grant the wisdom of the ages to anyone who could find it. However, it wasn't easy to obtain. The Golden

Pomegranate was guarded by riddles and tests of wisdom that only the cleverest of creatures could pass.

"Perhaps I am clever enough to find it," Kian thought to himself. "And with its wisdom, I can help my village even more."

So, with a heart full of determination, Kian set off on a journey towards the mountains. The sky was clear, and the sun shone brightly over the vast desert plains as he flew from village to village, asking the villagers for directions to the ancient temple where the Golden Pomegranate was said to grow. Finally, after days of flying over jagged cliffs and winding paths, Kian arrived at the foot of the towering mountains.

There, in the distance, he saw the golden glow of a temple perched high above the clouds. As he flew closer, a wise old raven appeared in front of him, blocking his path.

"You seek the Golden Pomegranate, little sparrow?" the raven croaked. "Many have tried to reach it, but none have passed the tests. Do you think you can succeed where others have failed?"

Kian, though small, puffed out his chest and nodded confidently. "I believe I can."

The raven's eyes gleamed with amusement. "Very well. You must answer my riddles. Fail, and you will never reach the temple. Are you ready?"

Kian nodded, and the raven began:

"I have cities, but no houses. I have forests, but no trees. I have rivers, but no water. What am I?"

Kian thought carefully. He had heard riddles like this before, but this one was tricky. He closed his eyes and imagined the world, the vast deserts, the green fields, the mountains, and the rivers. Then, it struck him.

"A map!" Kian chirped. "A map has cities but no houses, forests but no trees, and rivers but no water!"

The raven cawed in approval. "Correct! You have answered the first riddle. But there is more to come."

With that, the raven flew ahead, guiding Kian up the rocky path toward the temple. After hours of climbing, they reached the entrance, a grand stone doorway adorned with ancient carvings. The raven paused and spoke once more:

"I am tall when I am young and short when I am old. What am I?"

Kian tilted his head, thinking deeply. The answer came quickly, as if whispered by the wind.

"A candle!" Kian said confidently. "A candle is tall when it's new and short when it's burned down."

The raven's wings flapped, and he stepped aside. "Well done, little sparrow. You have answered both riddles correctly. You may enter."

With a flutter of excitement, Kian flew through the stone doorway and into the temple. Inside, the air was thick with the scent of pomegranate and jasmine. At the far end of the temple stood a massive tree—its trunk was silver, its branches spread wide, and on its lowest branch hung a single, glowing Golden Pomegranate.

As Kian approached the tree, a soft voice echoed through the temple:

"Who seeks the Golden Pomegranate?"

"I am Kian, the sparrow from the village below," Kian replied. "I seek the wisdom it promises."

The voice continued, "To obtain the Golden Pomegranate, you must show your wisdom. What is the most precious gift one can give to another?"

Kian paused. He had solved riddles, climbed mountains, and faced many challenges, but this was the most important question of all. *"What was the most precious gift?"*

He thought of the villagers, of his friends, and of all the times he had helped others. Then it came to him — the gift of kindness.

"The most precious gift is kindness," Kian said with certainty. "It costs nothing, yet it has the power to heal hearts, bring joy, and create lasting bonds."

The voice in the temple was silent for a long moment. Then it spoke, soft and deep:

"You have answered correctly, Kian. The wisdom of the Golden Pomegranate is yours."

The tree glowed brighter, and the Golden Pomegranate shimmered. Kian gently plucked the fruit from the branch and held it in his tiny claws. As he did, a wave of warmth and knowledge flooded his mind. He understood the value of sharing, of helping others without expecting anything in return, and the true meaning of wisdom.

With the Golden Pomegranate in his grasp, Kian flew back to his village, carrying its wisdom. He shared the fruit with the villagers, and they all learned from its lessons—kindness, generosity, and the importance of helping one another. The village flourished, and Kian became not just known for his cleverness, but for his wisdom and compassion.

Moral of The Story

The greatest wisdom lies in kindness and generosity. It is through helping others and sharing what we have that we grow the most.

Riddles*

- ❖ *"I have cities, but no houses. I have forests, but no trees. I have rivers, but no water. What am I?"*
- ❖ *"I am tall when I am young, and short when I am old. What am I?"*
- ❖ *"What was the most precious gift?"*

The Brave Turtle
and The Rainbow Stone
(A Story from Turkey)

Once upon a time, in a quaint village near the Aegean Sea in Turkey, there lived a young turtle named *Zeynep*. Zeynep was small, with a shell that shimmered in the sunlight, reflecting the colors of the world around her. Though she was known for her quiet nature, Zeynep harbored a deep desire to prove her courage. She had always been told that turtles were slow and cautious, but Zeynep dreamed of becoming more—of doing something extraordinary, just like the heroes in the stories the villagers would tell.

One evening, as Zeynep was sitting by the village well, she overheard two elders talking about the fabled Rainbow Stone. They spoke of its power to grant not only wisdom but also bravery to the one who could solve the puzzles guarding it. The stone was hidden deep within the enchanted valley, surrounded by mountains that no one had dared to cross. The elders said only those who were truly brave and wise could pass the tests and claim the Rainbow Stone.

Zeynep's heart swelled with excitement. *This* was the challenge she had been waiting for. Without hesitation, she decided to embark on a journey to find the Rainbow Stone.

The very next morning, Zeynep set off on her adventure. Her journey took her through thick forests, across streams, and up steep hills. Along the way, she met many animals—a wise old owl, a graceful deer, and a mischievous squirrel—but none could offer her help in finding the stone. She was on her own, but that only made Zeynep more determined.

Finally, after days of travel, Zeynep arrived at the entrance to the secret valley. There, at the base of a tall mountain, stood the fabled Rainbow Stone, glowing softly in the morning light. But guarding the stone was a fierce lion with golden eyes, who stood tall and proud.

"You wish to claim the Rainbow Stone?" the lion asked, his voice deep and echoing. "To do so, you must answer my riddles. Fail, and you will leave this valley empty-handed."

Zeynep nodded, her heart pounding with anticipation. She was ready for whatever challenge lay ahead.

The lion spoke the first riddle:

"I am not alive, but I grow; I do not have lungs, but I need air; I do not have a mouth, but water kills me. What am I?"

Zeynep closed her eyes and thought. She had seen many things in her travels—a flower, trees, the sky—but this riddle was trickier. She thought about it for a long time, and then it struck her.

"Fire!" Zeynep exclaimed, her voice clear. "Fire grows when it has air, but it can't survive in water."

The lion's golden eyes sparkled with approval. "Correct. You have passed the first riddle. But there is one more to solve."

The lion stepped aside, and before Zeynep stood the Rainbow Stone, its colors shifting in the light. But the lion's voice called out again:

"I can be cracked, made, told, and played. What am I?"

Zeynep thought for a moment. She had heard stories, shared laughter with her friends, and seen the joy of the village. The answer came to her quickly.

"It's a *joke*!" she said, her eyes bright. "A joke can be cracked, made, told, and played."

The lion stepped back, nodding in approval. "You have answered both riddles, little turtle. You have proven your wisdom and bravery. The Rainbow Stone is yours."

As Zeynep stepped forward to touch the Rainbow Stone, a warm light enveloped her, and she felt a surge of courage like never before. The stone had not only granted her wisdom, but it had also given her the bravery to believe in herself, no matter how small she seemed in the eyes of others. She felt ready to face any challenge that lay ahead.

With the Rainbow Stone in her possession, Zeynep returned to her village, where she was greeted as a hero. The villagers marveled at her bravery and wisdom, and Zeynep shared the lessons she had learned—the importance of thinking carefully, the power of laughter, and the strength that comes from believing in oneself.

From that day forward, Zeynep became a symbol of courage in her village. She showed everyone, young and old, that bravery doesn't come from size or strength, but from the heart. And though she was a turtle, she proved that even the smallest among us can achieve great things.

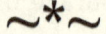

Moral of The Story

True bravery comes from within. It is not the size or strength of a person, but the courage to believe in oneself and to face challenges with wisdom and determination.

Riddles *

- ❖ *"I am not alive, but I grow; I do not have lungs, but I need air; I do not have a mouth, but water kills me. What am I?"*
- ❖ *"I can be cracked, made, told, and played. What am I?"*

The Brave Highland Deer
and The Stone of The Lost Clan
(A Story from Scotland)

Long ago, in the rolling hills of the Scottish Highlands, there lived a young deer named *Eòin* (pronounced "Owen"). Eòin was graceful and quick, his coat a rich chestnut color, blending seamlessly with the autumn leaves. Though the other deer of his herd were content to roam the valley and enjoy the quiet beauty of their lives, Eòin often dreamt of something greater — something beyond the peaceful glens and forests.

Eòin had heard old tales from the elder animals about the *Stone of the Lost Clan*, a mystical stone hidden deep in the highlands. It was said that whoever could solve the riddles inscribed on the stone would be granted the wisdom and strength to restore honor to their people. Many had tried to find the stone, but none had returned. The land was filled with legends of those who had ventured out in search of it — brave men and women, warriors, and kings — but the stone was elusive.

One evening, under a pale full moon, Eòin overheard an old owl named *Álainn* speaking to the foxes by the edge of the loch. The owl had seen the stone in her youth, but no one had laid eyes on it for generations.

"Only the bravest and wisest can find the Stone of the Lost Clan," Álainn said, her feathers ruffled by the evening breeze. "The riddles it asks are not for the faint of heart. If you seek it, know that your strength will be tested, but your mind will be tested even more."

Eòin's heart raced with excitement. He had always felt that he was destined for something more and this was his chance to prove it. The next morning, without a second thought, he set off into the highlands, determined to find the stone and unlock its ancient secrets.

For days, Eòin traveled through the misty forests and over the rocky hills, moving swiftly through the dense fog. The landscape around him was as beautiful as it was treacherous—sharp cliffs, rushing rivers, and towering trees that seemed to watch over him. But Eòin's determination never wavered. He knew that the path was difficult, but he believed that the stone was waiting for him.

Finally, after many days of travel, Eòin arrived at a hidden valley, where a large stone pillar stood at its center, glowing faintly in the dim light of dusk. The pillar was covered in ancient symbols, and at its base lay a deep, silent pool of water. As Eòin approached, he could feel the air grow still, as if the very valley was holding its breath.

A voice echoed from the stone, deep and rumbling:

"To claim the Stone of the Lost Clan, you must solve my riddles. Fail and you will never leave this valley. Succeed, and your clan shall be restored to glory. Are you ready?"

Eòin nodded firmly, his heart pounding but his mind sharp. The voice spoke the first riddle:

"I speak without a mouth and hear without ears. I have no body, but I come alive with the wind. What am I?"

Eòin thought carefully. He had heard stories of the wind singing through the trees, of the echoes that bounced off the mountain sides. After a moment, he smiled.

"It's an *echo*," Eòin said confidently. "An echo speaks without a mouth and hears without ears, and it comes alive when the wind carries it."

The voice was silent for a moment, and then it replied:

"Correct. Now, for the second riddle."

The stone's glow brightened, and the air around Eòin seemed to hum with anticipation. The voice continued:

"The more of this there is, the less you see. What am I?"

Eòin blinked, thinking back to the thick fog that often rolled over the hills and made it difficult to see. The answer came to him quickly.

"It's *darkness*," he said. "The more darkness there is, the less you can see."

The voice, now softer and warmer, said, "You have passed both riddles, brave deer. The Stone of the Lost Clan is yours."

With that, the stone began to glow brightly, illuminating the entire valley. A brilliant light filled the air, and Eòin felt a surge of energy and clarity. He could feel the wisdom of the land, the strength of the mountains, and the pulse of the ancient clans filling him with purpose.

The stone lifted from the ground, and as it did, the valley seemed to transform. The once-hidden glen became vibrant, alive with the beauty of new life. Eòin, now filled with the wisdom and courage of his ancestors, knew what he had to do.

He returned to his herd, where he shared the lessons of the stone — the importance of wisdom and unity, the strength of the heart, and the power of courage. His herd, once quiet and content, began to see the world through new eyes. They faced challenges with renewed strength, and soon, the entire valley flourished, its clans restored to their former glory.

And so, Eòin the deer became a legend. Not just for his bravery, but for the wisdom he brought to his people. He taught them that true strength does not come from size or speed, but from the courage to face challenges with a wise heart and an unwavering spirit.

Moral of The Story

True bravery is not only about strength; it is about wisdom and knowing when to use your courage to do what is right. A brave heart and a clear mind can accomplish great things.

Riddles*

- ❖ *"I speak without a mouth and hear without ears. I have no body, but I come alive with the wind. What am I?"*
- ❖ *"The more of this there is, the less you see. What am I?"*

Find the answer to the riddle in the back of the book.

The Mountain Fox and The Heart
of The Northern Lights
(A Story from Norway)

In the northernmost reaches of Norway, where the sun barely touched the horizon in winter, there lived a young fox named *Sigrid*. With fur as white as the snow and eyes bright like the stars above, Sigrid was known for her keen mind and adventurous spirit. Though the other animals in the forest were content with the quiet life, Sigrid dreamed of something more—of adventure, of mystery, and of the ancient treasures hidden deep within the mountains.

One cold winter evening, while resting by the edge of a frozen lake, Sigrid overheard an old raven named *Viggo* telling tales to a group of curious owls. He spoke of a legendary treasure, *the Heart of the Northern Lights*, a magical gem that could grant the wisdom of the ages and the strength to face any challenge. But the Heart was hidden deep within the mountains, guarded by riddles and ancient spirits that only the bravest could overcome.

Intrigued by the idea of such a treasure, Sigrid's heart raced with excitement. She knew that if she could find the Heart, it would grant her the courage and wisdom she needed to protect her forest home and help the animals around her. So, without hesitation, she set out on a journey to find the elusive gem.

The journey was long and treacherous. Sigrid traveled across frozen rivers, climbed steep hills, and trekked through snowstorms so fierce that the world seemed to disappear behind a wall of white. Yet, with every challenge she faced, Sigrid grew more determined. She was guided by the flickering glow of the Northern Lights, which shimmered in the night sky, casting an ethereal light over the snowy landscape.

After many days, Sigrid reached the base of a towering mountain, its peak hidden in the 8swirling mists. At the foot of the mountain, she found a stone archway, covered in ancient runes. As she approached, a deep voice echoed through the air, sending a chill down her spine.

"Who dares seek the Heart of the Northern Lights?" the voice boomed.

"I am Sigrid, the mountain fox," she replied bravely, her voice steady despite her nervousness. "I seek the Heart to gain wisdom and courage."

The voice responded with a riddle:

"I have keys but open no doors. I have space but no room. I have a face but no features. What am I?"

Sigrid's mind raced. She had heard many riddles before, but this one was tricky. She closed her eyes, imagining the world around her — thinking of the snow-covered trees, the silent mountains, and the glowing lights above. Then, the answer came to her.

"It's a *keyboard*," she said, her voice confident. "A keyboard has keys, but it doesn't open doors. It has space but no room, and it has a face but no features."

The voice was silent for a moment before speaking again, softer this time.

"Correct, Sigrid. But one riddle remains. Solve it, and the Heart of the Northern Lights will be yours."

The mist swirled around her as the voice asked the second riddle:

"I can be cracked, I can be made, I can be told, and I can be played. What am I?"

Sigrid thought carefully. She had heard many tales of laughter and mischief from the animals in her forest, and the answer was clear to her now.

"It's a *joke*," she said with a smile. "A joke can be cracked, made, told, and played."

The mountain trembled, and a soft glow appeared at the top of the peak. The mist cleared, revealing a hidden cave, where the Heart of the Northern Lights lay on a pedestal made of stone. The gem was a brilliant sapphire, glowing with a light that seemed to dance like the aurora itself.

As Sigrid approached, she could feel the power of the gem. When she touched it, warmth flooded her body, and she could feel the wisdom of the ages coursing through her veins. She understood the balance of nature, the power of the stars, and the secrets of the ancient forest. The Heart had granted her not only wisdom but also the courage to face any danger that might threaten her home.

With the Heart of the Northern Lights in her possession, Sigrid returned to her forest, where the animals greeted her as a hero. She used the wisdom she had gained to help the forest thrive, guiding the animals through harsh winters and ensuring that the balance of nature was preserved. She shared the lessons of bravery, wisdom, and unity with all, and the forest flourished as never before.

Sigrid the mountain fox became a legend in the land, known not only for her courage but for the light she brought to the lives of those around her. And though the Northern Lights continued to dance across the sky, it was Sigrid's heart, now filled with wisdom and courage that shone the brightest.

Moral of The Story

True bravery comes from within. With wisdom and courage, you can overcome any challenge and find the strength to help others.

Riddles *

- ❖ *"I have keys but open no doors. I have space but no room. I have a face but no features. What am I?"*
- ❖ *"I can be cracked, I can be made, I can be told, I can be played. What am I?"*

*Find the answer to the riddle in the back of the book.

The Clever Crane and The Jade Emperor's Secret
(A Story from China)

Long ago, in a small village nestled in the shadow of the misty mountains of China, there lived a graceful and intelligent crane named *Meilin*. Meilin was known throughout the village for her wisdom and kindness. She was a friend to everyone, often helping the villagers with their daily tasks and offering advice whenever they needed it. But despite her happiness, Meilin always felt there was more to learn, a deeper truth about the world that she had yet to discover.

One crisp morning, as Meilin flew over the village, she overheard an old storyteller speaking to a group of curious children. He spoke of the *Jade Emperor*, the ruler of the heavens, and the *Mirror of the Sky*, a magical mirror hidden deep within the mountains. The mirror, the storyteller said, could reveal the truth of one's heart and grant wisdom beyond measure. But only those who could solve the three riddles set by the Jade Emperor himself could find it.

The story filled Meilin with a sense of wonder. She had long felt that her purpose was greater than the peaceful life she led in the village. Perhaps the Mirror of the Sky could help her discover the wisdom she sought.

Determined, Meilin set off on a journey toward the mountains. Her wings cut through the cool morning air as she flew over forests, rivers, and high cliffs, guided by the stars above. Along the way, she met many animals—an old turtle, a mischievous monkey, and a wise owl—but none of them knew the way to the Jade Emperor's secret garden.

After many days of travel, Meilin finally reached the entrance to the mystical garden. The path was lined with jade stones that shimmered in the sunlight, and the air smelled sweet with the fragrance of blooming lotus flowers. But as she ventured deeper into the garden, a large stone gate appeared, guarded by a golden lion with glowing eyes.

The lion spoke in a deep, resonant voice: "Who seeks the Mirror of the Sky? Only those who are wise of heart and sharp of mind may pass."

"I am Meilin, the crane," she said, bowing respectfully. "I seek the Mirror of the Sky to learn the wisdom of the world."

The lion's eyes gleamed as it spoke the first riddle:

"I speak without a mouth and hear without ears. I have no body, but I come alive with the wind. What am I?"

Meilin paused, her mind focused. She had heard this riddle before in her youth, and it was a simple one. She smiled and replied confidently:

"It's an *echo*. An echo speaks without a mouth, hears without ears, and comes alive with the wind."

The lion nodded in approval and stepped aside. "Correct, Meilin. One riddle remains."

Meilin continued down the path, feeling the weight of her journey. She passed through a grove of ancient trees, their trunks twisted with age, until she reached a small clearing. There, she found a second guardian—an enormous jade serpent, its scales glimmering like emeralds.

The serpent hissed softly, and in a voice that seemed to come from the very earth, it asked the second riddle:

"The more you take, the more you leave behind. What am I?"

Meilin thought carefully. This riddle was trickier, but she was determined. She pictured the steps she had taken on her journey, the path she had followed through the forest. And then, the answer came to her.

"Its *footsteps*," she said. "The more footsteps you take, the more you leave behind."

The serpent's eyes flickered with approval, and it slithered back into the shadows. "Well done, Meilin. You have answered both riddles correctly. The final test awaits."

As Meilin ventured deeper into the garden, the sky began to darken, and the air became thick with the scent of jasmine. At the end of the path stood the grand temple where the Mirror of the Sky was said to reside. There, in front of the temple, stood an old, wise tortoise with a shell that sparkled like the stars.

The tortoise spoke with a voice full of wisdom: "Only those who understand the heart's true nature may gaze upon the Mirror of the Sky. Solve my final riddle, and the mirror will reveal itself to you."

Meilin bowed her head, listening carefully as the tortoise spoke:

"I am always in front of you, but I can never be seen. I am your greatest ally, yet I am invisible. What am I?"

Meilin closed her eyes and took a deep breath. She thought of everything she had learned on her journey, the wisdom of the land, the wind beneath her wings, and the gentle songs of the rivers. Then, she realized the answer.

"It's *the future*," Meilin said. "The future is always ahead of us, but we can never see it. It is our greatest ally because it holds the possibilities of all that we can become, yet it remains invisible."

The tortoise smiled, its ancient eyes twinkling. "You have answered wisely, Meilin. The Mirror of the Sky is yours to behold."

As the tortoise spoke, the ground beneath her feet began to shimmer, and the Mirror of the Sky appeared before her, glowing with a soft, ethereal light. Meilin stepped forward, gazing into the mirror. As she looked into the reflection, she saw not just her own face, but the faces of all the creatures she had helped along her journey. The mirror revealed her heart—a heart full of kindness, courage, and wisdom.

Meilin realized then that the greatest wisdom was not in knowing the future or solving riddles, but in understanding that the heart's true strength lies in its ability to help others.

With the Mirror's wisdom, Meilin returned to her village, where she shared her newfound understanding with the animals and people alike. And though the Mirror of the Sky remained hidden in the mountains, Meilin carried its wisdom with her always.

Moral of The Story

True wisdom comes from understanding the heart. It is not about knowing the future or solving every riddle, but about helping others and using your knowledge for the greater good.

Riddles*

- ❖ *"I speak without a mouth and hear without ears. I have no body, but I come alive with the wind. What am I?"*
- ❖ *"The more you take, the more you leave behind. What am I?"*
- ❖ *"I am always in front of you, but I can never be seen. I am your greatest ally, yet I am invisible. What am I?"*

*Find the answer to the riddle in the back of the book.

The Lion and The Golden Horn

(A Story from Ethiopia)

Long ago, in the rich and fertile lands of Ethiopia, there lived a young lion named *Tewodros*. Tewodros was strong and courageous, respected by the animals of the savanna. He ruled his pride with fairness and strength, but there was something missing in his heart—something he could not understand. Despite his strength, he often felt uncertain in moments of great responsibility. He wondered if there was more to being a leader than just power.

One evening, as the stars began to twinkle in the sky, Tewodros sat by the edge of a quiet river. An old wise baboon named *Bako*, known for his knowledge of the ancient ways, approached him. Bako had lived many years and had traveled far, learning the secrets of the land.

"Why do you look so troubled, young lion?" asked Bako.

Tewodros sighed deeply. "I am strong, but sometimes I feel unsure of myself. I want to be a wise leader, someone my pride can look up to, but I do not know how."

Bako smiled kindly, his eyes gleaming. "There is a place, deep in the highlands, where the Golden Horn rests. It is said that whoever can find it and answer the riddles of the spirits will be granted wisdom, strength, and the heart of a true leader. It is not an easy journey, but it may be the answer you seek."

Determined to become the leader his pride needed, Tewodros set off the very next day. His journey led him across sweeping plains, through dense forests, and up rugged mountains. The higher he climbed, the colder the air became, and the challenges grew harder. But Tewodros pressed on, his heart set on finding the Golden

Horn and unlocking the wisdom that would help him rule with both strength and fairness.

Finally, after many days of travel, Tewodros reached the entrance to a secret valley. The ground shimmered with golden dust, and the air hummed with an ancient energy. At the center of the valley stood a majestic tree with branches that stretched toward the sky. Beneath the tree lay a beautiful golden horn, glowing with a soft, ethereal light. But guarding it was a great spirit — a lioness, her coat as silver as the moon, her eyes wise and knowing.

"You have come to seek the Golden Horn," the lioness said, her voice deep and full of ancient wisdom. "But to claim it, you must answer three riddles. Fail, and you will leave empty-handed. Succeed, and you will gain the wisdom and strength to be a true leader."

Tewodros nodded, ready for whatever lay ahead. The lioness spoke the first riddle:

"I can fill a room, but I take up no space. What am I?"

Tewodros thought carefully, remembering the many times he had sat in the savanna with his pride, hearing the sounds of nature all around. Then, the answer came to him.

"It's *light*," he said confidently. "Light can fill a room, but it takes up no physical space."

The lioness nodded, her eyes glowing with approval. "Correct. You have passed the first test. Now, for the second."

The lioness raised her paw, and the ground around them shifted, revealing a vast desert stretching out before Tewodros. The heat was intense, but the lioness's voice rang clear.

"I am always hungry; I must always be fed. The finger I touch will soon turn red. What am I?"

Tewodros's mind raced. He had seen many things in his life, but this riddle was trickier. He thought of the many dangers in the wild, the things that could cause pain. And then, he realized the answer.

"It's *fire*," Tewodros said, his voice steady. "Fire is always hungry, always needing fuel, and anything it touches will burn."

The lioness smiled, and the desert disappeared, replaced by a peaceful green meadow. "You have answered wisely. One more riddle remains."

Tewodros stood tall, feeling the weight of the final test. The lioness spoke the last riddle:

"The more you take, the more you leave behind. What am I?"

Tewodros thought deeply, remembering the long journey he had taken. He reflected on the many steps he had made and the distances he had traveled. The answer came to him clearly.

"It's *footsteps*," he said. "The more steps you take, the more you leave behind."

The lioness's eyes gleamed with pride. "You have answered all three riddles, young lion. You have proven that you possess both the strength of body and the wisdom of mind. The Golden Horn is yours."

With a graceful movement, the lioness stepped aside, allowing Tewodros to claim the Golden Horn. As he touched it, a warm, golden light enveloped him. The wisdom and strength of countless leaders from the past filled his heart and mind. He now understood that true leadership was not just about strength—it was about wisdom, humility, and understanding the needs of others.

With the Golden Horn in his possession, Tewodros returned to his pride. When he arrived, his pride was amazed at the change in him. He no longer ruled through fear, but with compassion and wisdom. His heart was as strong as his body, and his leadership brought prosperity and peace to his pride.

Tewodros's journey became a legend, told for generations to come. He had proven that the greatest leaders are not those who are strongest in battle, but those who are wise and just, understanding the hearts of those they lead.

Moral of The Story

True strength lies not only in physical power but in the wisdom, humility, and understanding needed to lead others. A great leader listens, learns, and leads with a kind heart.

Riddles *

- ❖ *"I can fill a room, but I take up no space. What am I?"*
- ❖ *"I am always hungry; I must always be fed. The finger I touch, will soon turn red. What am I?"*
- ❖ *"The more you take, the more you leave behind. What am I?"*

The Jaguar and The Spirit
of The Amazon
(A Story from Brazil)

Long ago, in the dense jungles of Brazil, there lived a young jaguar named *Iara*. She was known throughout the forest for her swift movements, keen senses, and powerful presence. Yet, despite her strength, Iara often felt that something was missing—she longed to become not just a strong and capable hunter, but a wise leader who could guide the animals of the forest through both danger and peace. But she wasn't sure how to gain this wisdom.

One day, while hunting near the riverbank, Iara overheard a conversation between two parrots perched in the trees. They spoke of a legendary spirit that resided in a hidden clearing deep within the jungle. This spirit, known as the *Spirit of the Amazon*, was said to possess the knowledge of the entire rainforest. Whoever could find the spirit and pass its trials would be granted both wisdom and the heart of a true leader.

Intrigued and determined to grow into the leader her forest needed, Iara decided to embark on the perilous journey to find the Spirit of the Amazon. She would need courage, cunning, and strength to face the challenges ahead.

The journey was not an easy one. Iara had to navigate the thick underbrush, cross fast-moving rivers, and climb towering trees. Along the way, she encountered various animals—some kind, some curious, and others who tried to trick her. But Iara pressed on, her heart filled with purpose.

Finally, after many days, Iara reached the clearing. It was a place of great beauty: ancient trees surrounded a shimmering pool, and the air was thick with the scent of blooming orchids. In the center of the pool stood a tall stone pillar, atop which rested a golden mask, glinting in the sunlight.

At that moment, a soft voice filled the air, and from the shadows emerged a glowing figure — the Spirit of the Amazon. The spirit was an ethereal being, neither fully human nor animal, with eyes that sparkled like the stars and a presence that seemed to pulse with the energy of the entire rainforest.

"You seek wisdom, young jaguar," the spirit said. "But wisdom is not given freely. You must prove yourself by answering three riddles. Fail, and you will leave empty-handed. Succeed, and you will gain the strength and knowledge you seek."

Iara bowed respectfully. "I am ready. Please, ask your riddles."

The spirit nodded and spoke the first riddle:

"I have cities, but no houses. I have forests, but no trees. I have rivers, but no water. What am I?"

Iara thought for a moment. She had seen maps drawn by the humans who sometimes wandered the jungle, and the answer became clear.

"It's a *map*," Iara said confidently. "A map has cities, forests, and rivers, but none of them are real — they are just representations."

The spirit's eyes gleamed with approval. "Correct. But the next riddle is more difficult."

With a flick of its hand, the spirit summoned a gust of wind, and the clearing was suddenly filled with the sound of rustling leaves. The spirit spoke again:

"I am always in front of you, but you can never see me. I am the key to your future, yet I am always hidden. What am I?"

Iara felt a chill in the air and thought of the many paths that lay before her in life. Then, the answer came to her.

"It's the *future*," she said. "The future is always ahead of us, but we cannot see it. It is hidden, yet it is what drives us forward."

The spirit smiled, its form shimmering like the mist. "You are wise, young jaguar. But one more test remains."

The spirit raised its hand, and a great storm began to swirl around Iara. The wind howled, and the rain poured, but the jaguar stood firm, her body steady and her mind focused.

The final riddle was spoken in a deep, rumbling voice:

"The more you take, the more you leave behind. What am I?"

Iara thought deeply, remembering the journey she had just completed. She had taken many steps through the jungle, each one leading her closer to the clearing. The answer was clear.

"It's *footsteps*," she said. "The more steps you take, the more you leave behind."

The storm ceased, and the jungle became calm once more. The Spirit of the Amazon stepped forward, its light shining brightly.

"You have answered all three riddles with wisdom and clarity, young jaguar," the spirit said. "You are now ready to be the leader you seek to be."

With a wave of its hand, the spirit lifted the golden mask from the pillar and placed it upon Iara's head. In an instant, Iara felt a surge of understanding flow through her—she could now hear the whispers of the forest, understand the needs of every animal, and guide her pride with both strength and compassion. The Spirit of the Amazon had granted her the wisdom she sought.

Iara returned to her jungle, now a leader in every sense of the word. She used her newfound knowledge to protect her forest home, guiding the animals through every season with fairness and care. Under her leadership, the jungle thrived, and Iara's name became a legend in the Amazon.

From that day on, the jungle knew peace, for Iara had learned that true leadership comes not from strength alone, but from wisdom, compassion, and a deep understanding of those you lead.

Moral Of The Story

True leadership is a balance of strength and wisdom. To lead with heart, one must first understand and listen to those they are meant to guide.

Riddles *

- ❖ *"I have cities, but no houses. I have forests, but no trees. I have rivers, but no water. What am I?"*
- ❖ *"I am always in front of you, but you can never see me. I am the key to your future, yet I am always hidden. What am I?"*
- ❖ *"The more you take, the more you leave behind. What am I?"*

Find the answer to the riddle in the back of the book.

The Crane and The Hidden Pond

(A Story from Japan)

Long ago, in a peaceful village nestled at the foot of the mountains, there lived a young crane named *Sora*. Sora was graceful and swift, admired by all the animals of the forest. Yet, despite her beauty and agility, she often felt that something was missing. She longed to discover the true purpose of her life, to learn what it meant to live with wisdom and kindness, and to help her friends in a deeper way.

One morning, as the sun rose over the mountain peaks, Sora overheard an old tortoise telling a group of children a story. He spoke of a hidden pond deep in the forest, guarded by spirits of nature. It was said that whoever could find the pond and answer its riddles would gain the wisdom to live with true understanding. But the journey was difficult, and only those with pure hearts could find their way.

Sora, filled with both curiosity and hope, decided to embark on the journey. She spread her wings and flew high into the sky, following the whispering winds that seemed to guide her toward the heart of the forest. Her journey took her across valleys, over rivers, and through thick bamboo groves. Along the way, she met many animals—a wise fox, a playful squirrel, and an old owl—all of whom had heard of the pond but could not find it themselves.

After many days, Sora finally reached the entrance to the hidden forest. The trees here were ancient, their branches heavy with the weight of time. The air was thick with the scent of pine and moss, and the sounds of the forest seemed to grow quieter as if waiting for something to happen. In the center of the forest was the pond, its surface smooth and still, like a mirror reflecting the sky above. But beside the pond stood a great stone gate, and on it were inscribed three riddles.

Before she could approach, a spirit appeared — an elegant white deer, her antlers glowing softly in the moonlight. The deer spoke in a gentle voice:

"You seek wisdom, young crane. But to gain it, you must first prove yourself worthy. Answer the three riddles of the pond, and you will be granted the knowledge you seek. Fail, and you must leave this place forever."

Sora nodded bravely. "I am ready. Please, ask your riddles."

The deer's eyes gleamed, and she spoke the first riddle:

"The more you take, the more you leave behind. What am I?"

Sora thought for a moment, recalling all the steps she had taken on her journey. She had passed through fields, climbed hills, and crossed rivers, always leaving something behind. And then it came to her.

"Its *footsteps*," Sora said. "The more steps you take, the more you leave behind."

The deer nodded, and the stone gate opened, revealing a path that led deeper into the forest. "Correct. But the next riddle awaits."

Sora continued on the path, her heart filled with determination. After walking for a short while, the deer spoke again:

"I have keys but open no doors. I have space but no room. You can enter, but you can't go outside. What am I?"

Sora paused, feeling the weight of the riddle. She thought of the many things she had encountered on her journey, and then the answer appeared in her mind.

"It's a *piano*," she said. "A piano has keys, but they don't open doors. It has space inside, but no room to go through. You can enter a song, but you can't go outside of it."

The deer smiled, and the path before Sora seemed to shimmer with a soft glow. "Well done. You are one step closer to wisdom. But there is one last riddle."

Sora, though tired, pressed on, knowing that the final test was near. She reached a quiet clearing where the deer waited, her antlers glowing brighter than ever. The final riddle was spoken in a soft voice:

"I can be cracked, I can be made, I can be told, I can be played. What am I?"

Sora thought deeply. She had heard many stories in her life, and her mind raced with possibilities. Then, the answer came to her clearly.

"It's a *joke*," she said. "A joke can be cracked, made, told, and played."

The deer's eyes sparkled with joy. "You have answered all the riddles correctly, young crane. You have proven yourself worthy."

As Sora gazed into the pond, she saw not just her own reflection, but the reflections of all the animals she had met along her journey — each one with their own strengths, hopes, and dreams. The pond had shown her something important: true wisdom is not about knowing everything, but understanding that everyone has something valuable to share, and that each journey, no matter how long or difficult, is part of the path to wisdom.

The deer bowed to Sora. "You have found the wisdom you sought. Now, you may return to your home with a heart full of understanding."

With a heart lighter than ever before, Sora flew back to her village, her wings now filled with a deeper purpose. She helped the other animals of the forest with new insights and understanding, teaching them that true wisdom comes from listening, learning, and sharing.

And so, the crane became not only a graceful creature of the sky but also a wise guide to all who sought her counsel in the peaceful forests of Japan.

Moral of The Story

True wisdom comes from understanding that learning is a lifelong journey. It is about listening, sharing, and embracing the lessons of those around you. Every step, every person, and every experience contributes to a deeper understanding of the world.

Riddles *

- ❖ *"The more you take, the more you leave behind. What am I?"*
- ❖ *"I have keys but open no doors. I have space but no room. You can enter, but you can't go outside. What am I?"*
- ❖ *"I can be cracked, I can be made, I can be told, I can be played. What am I?"*

Find the answer to the riddle in the back of the book.

The Coconut and The Wise Owl
(A Story from Cuba)

In a small village nestled near the shores of Cuba, there lived a young and curious parrot named *Paco*. Paco was known for his bright feathers, quick wit, and loud, cheerful voice. He loved to talk and explore, always eager to learn something new. But despite his sharp mind, Paco often felt that there was more to life than just learning facts. He longed for true wisdom — a wisdom that would help him makes his village a better place for everyone.

One sunny afternoon, while flying over the beach, Paco overheard an old owl named *Abuelo* talking to a group of children by the water. Abuelo was the oldest and wisest creature in the village. His feathers were grey with age, and his eyes sparkled with the knowledge of years gone by. He spoke of an ancient lagoon hidden deep within the jungle, where the *Spirit of the Island* resided. The spirit, he said, would grant wisdom to anyone who could solve the three riddles guarding the lagoon. Many had tried to find the lagoon, but only a few had succeeded, and those who did returned as leaders of great wisdom.

Paco's heart raced with excitement. He knew he had to find this lagoon and uncover the wisdom he sought. With determination, he flapped his wings and set off toward the jungle, guided by the whispers of the wind and the stories he had heard from the elders.

The path to the lagoon was not an easy one. Paco flew over thick canopies of trees, through tangled vines, and across rushing rivers. Along the way, he encountered various animals who tried to deter him, but Paco's spirit remained strong. After days of travel, Paco finally reached the edge of the jungle, where the trees parted to reveal a serene lagoon shimmering under the midday sun. In the center of the lagoon stood a large rock with a smooth surface, upon which were etched three mysterious riddles.

At the water's edge, Paco saw Abuelo, the wise owl, perched on a branch overlooking the pond. His feathers glowed in the dappled sunlight as he spoke.

"You have come, young parrot," Abuelo said in a deep, soothing voice. "To gain the wisdom you seek, you must answer the three riddles of the lagoon. If you answer correctly, you will be granted the wisdom to guide others. But be warned—if you fail, you will have to leave this place forever."

Paco nodded eagerly. "I am ready, Abuelo. Please ask the riddles."

Abuelo's wise eyes sparkled as he spoke the first riddle:

"I have keys but open no doors. I have space but no room. You can enter, but you can't go outside. What am I?"

Paco thought for a moment. He had seen many things in his life, but the answer was elusive. Then, his eyes brightened as he remembered something.

"I know the answer! It's a *piano*," Paco exclaimed. "A piano has keys, but they don't open doors. It has space inside, but no room to go through. And you can play music, but you can't escape from the song once it starts."

Abuelo nodded, pleased with Paco's answer. "Correct. You are wise beyond your years. But the next riddle awaits."

The owl's ancient voice filled the air as he spoke again:

"I am always with you, but you cannot see me. I guide you, but you cannot touch me. I can be heard, but I cannot be held. What am I?"

Paco's mind raced. He thought of all the things he had encountered in his travels, but nothing seemed to fit. Then, the answer came to him like a bird taking flight.

"It's *your voice*," Paco said. "Your voice is always with you, even if you can't see it. It guides you when you speak, but you can't touch it. And though it can be heard, it cannot be held."

Abuelo smiled again, his eyes full of pride. "Well done, young parrot. You are truly a sharp thinker. But there is one final riddle."

With a gentle movement, Abuelo pointed to the water of the lagoon, where the final riddle appeared written in the ripples:

"The more you have of me, the less you see. What am I?"

Paco stared at the water, puzzled. He had seen many things in his life, but this riddle seemed especially tricky. The answer wasn't clear, but he remembered something he had learned from the village elders—the importance of balance and moderation. Then, like the turning of a leaf in the wind, the answer came to him.

"It's *darkness*," Paco said with certainty. "The more darkness you have, the less you can see. Darkness hides things from view."

Abuelo nodded approvingly. "You have answered all three riddles correctly, young parrot. You have shown great wisdom and understanding. The spirit of the lagoon grants you the wisdom you sought."

With a soft ripple in the water, the lagoon shimmered, and Paco felt a wave of understanding wash over him. The wisdom he had gained was not just knowledge of facts, but an understanding of the balance in life, the importance of listening, and the need for patience and kindness in every decision.

As Paco flew back to the village, he felt different—stronger, wiser, and more compassionate. He shared the lessons he had learned with the animals of the village, teaching them the importance of thinking before acting, of helping one another, and of finding harmony with nature. The village flourished under his guidance, and Paco became a beloved leader known not just for his sharp mind, but for his deep wisdom and kindness.

Moral of The Story

True wisdom is not just about knowing things—it is about understanding the world and finding balance. A wise leader listens, learns, and helps others with compassion and thoughtfulness.

Riddles *

- ❖ *"I have keys but open no doors. I have space but no room. You can enter, but you can't go outside. What am I?"*
- ❖ *"I am always with you, but you cannot see me. I guide you, but you cannot touch me. I can be heard, but I cannot be held. What am I?"*
- ❖ *"The more you have of me, the less you see. What am I?"*

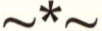

Find the answer to the riddle in the back of the book.

The Bamboo and The Clever Monkey
(A Story from Vietnam)

In a small village nestled between the hills and the river, there lived a young and playful monkey named *Ming*. Ming was known for his quick thinking, his boundless energy, and his love for solving puzzles. He was always the first to find clever solutions to tricky situations, and the other animals in the village often came to him for help. But Ming had a secret — despite all his cleverness, he felt like something was missing in his life. He longed for wisdom, not just intelligence, to understand the world more deeply and to help his friends even more.

One day, while playing in the bamboo forest, Ming overheard an old and wise owl named *Linh* telling a group of animals a story. Linh, with her soft feathers and sharp eyes, spoke of an ancient tree deep in the jungle, known as the *Tree of Wisdom*. It was said that anyone who could solve the three riddles of the tree would be granted knowledge to live a better life and lead others with kindness and clarity. However, the riddles were not easy, and many had tried and failed to find the tree's hidden wisdom.

Ming's heart raced with excitement. He knew this was the opportunity he had been waiting for. He wanted to find the tree, answer the riddles, and gain the wisdom to become a better friend and leader. With a determined heart, he set off on his journey.

The journey to find the Tree of Wisdom was long and difficult. Ming climbed steep mountains, crossed fast-flowing rivers, and ventured through dark, dense forests. Along the way, he met many animals who warned him that the riddles were not to be taken lightly. But Ming was confident and eager to prove himself. After several days of travel, he finally reached a clearing where the Tree of Wisdom stood. Its branches reached high into the sky, and its leaves shimmered in the sunlight as if they were made of gold.

At the base of the tree stood Linh, the wise owl, her eyes glowing with gentle warmth.

"You have made it, young monkey," Linh said, her voice echoing softly through the air. "To gain the wisdom you seek, you must solve three riddles. Answer correctly, and you will receive the knowledge to guide others with your heart. Fail, and you must leave this place."

Ming nodded eagerly. "I am ready, Linh. Please ask the riddles."

Linh's eyes twinkled as she spoke the first riddle:

"I am always hungry, I must always be fed. The finger I touch, will soon turn red. What am I?"

Ming thought for a moment, pondering the riddle. He had seen many things in his life, but the answer was still unclear. Then, he remembered the crackling fires he had seen in the village, and the warmth they provided on cold nights.

"I know the answer! It's *fire*," Ming said confidently. "Fire is always hungry because it needs fuel, and when you touch it, it can burn and turn your finger red."

Linh nodded approvingly. "Correct, young monkey. You are on the right path. But the next riddle awaits."

The owl's voice was calm and measured as she spoke the second riddle:

"The more you take, the more you leave behind. What am I?"

Ming thought hard. He had seen many animals move through the jungle, leaving tracks behind them, but nothing seemed to fit the riddle completely. Then, it struck him—he had been moving through the forest, and the answer was clear.

"It's *footsteps*," Ming said. "The more steps you take, the more you leave behind as you walk."

Linh smiled softly. "Well done, Ming. You are indeed clever. But there is one final riddle."

With a serene glance, Linh gestured to the branches of the Tree of Wisdom. The last riddle appeared in the air, glowing softly:

"I have keys but open no doors. I have space but no room. You can enter, but you can't go outside. What am I?"

Ming took a deep breath. This one was tricky. He thought about all the things he had seen in his travels and the things that seemed to fit the description. Finally, he remembered something he had played with in the village: a piano.

"It's *a piano*," Ming said. "A piano has keys, but they don't open doors. It has space inside, but no room to enter. You can play it, but you can't walk inside it."

Linh's eyes sparkled with approval. "You have answered all the riddles correctly, Ming. You have shown wisdom beyond your years. The Tree of Wisdom grants you the knowledge you sought."

With those words, the Tree of Wisdom shimmered, and Ming felt a gentle warmth fill his heart. He realized that true wisdom was not just about being clever—it was about understanding the needs of others, listening with an open heart, and acting with kindness. The wisdom was about balance, about knowing when to speak and when to listen, when to lead and when to follow.

As Ming made his way back to the village, he felt a new sense of purpose. He shared the wisdom he had gained with the other animals, teaching them that cleverness alone was not enough; they needed to care for each other and think about the world in a deeper way. The village prospered under Ming's guidance, and he became known not only for his cleverness but for his wisdom and compassion.

Moral of The Story

True wisdom is about more than intelligence. It's about understanding the world around you, listening to others, and showing kindness and balance in all your actions. Wisdom comes from the heart, and it helps us make better decisions and guide others with compassion.

Riddles *

- ❖ *"I am always hungry, I must always be fed. The finger I touch, will soon turn red. What am I?"*
- ❖ *"The more you take, the more you leave behind. What am I?"*
- ❖ *"I have keys but open no doors. I have space but no room. You can enter, but you can't go outside. What am I?"*

Find the answer to the riddle in the back of the book.

The Great Northern Lights
and The Brave Beaver
(A Story from Canada)

In the heart of the snowy Canadian wilderness, there lived a young and determined beaver named *Tansi*. Tansi was known for his strong work ethic, building dams and lodges like no one else in the village. He had sharp teeth, a sturdy tail, and a heart full of ambition. But despite his skill in building and working, Tansi always felt that there was something missing. He wanted to be wise, to understand the world and how to make the best decisions. He longed for the guidance that came from true wisdom, not just hard work.

One frosty morning, as Tansi was working on a new dam by the river, an old moose named *Wabigoon* passed by. Wabigoon had lived many winters and was known for his deep knowledge of the land. His antlers were wide and his movements slow, but his eyes gleamed with wisdom. He stopped by the dam and looked at Tansi thoughtfully.

"The Northern Lights are calling, young beaver," Wabigoon said in a voice that was both kind and mysterious. "They say that anyone who seeks their wisdom must solve three riddles hidden in the land and the sky. The answers will not only make you wise, but also teach you the balance of nature."

Tansi's heart skipped a beat. The Northern Lights, those beautiful, shimmering curtains of light in the sky, were said to hold the wisdom of the world. Tansi decided that he would seek the Northern Lights and uncover their secrets. With a brave heart, he packed a small bundle of food and set off on his journey.

The journey was not easy. Tansi traveled through snowy forests, climbed icy hills, and crossed frozen lakes. He met wolves, owls, and squirrels along the way, all of whom warned him about the difficulty of the riddles. But Tansi was determined. Finally, after many days, he reached the top of a tall mountain where the Northern Lights danced across the sky in all their glory.

At the peak of the mountain, standing beneath the shimmering lights, was Wabigoon the moose. His silhouette was outlined against the colorful sky, his presence peaceful and grand.

"You have come far, young beaver," Wabigoon said softly. "To gain the wisdom you seek, you must answer the three riddles. If you answer correctly, you will understand the true balance of life. Fail, and you will return without the wisdom you long for."

Tansi nodded, his heart full of determination. "I am ready, Wabigoon. Please, ask the riddles."

Wabigoon's voice rang out like the wind through the trees as he spoke the first riddle:

"I have cities, but no houses. I have forests, but no trees. I have rivers, but no water. What am I?"

Tansi thought hard. He had seen maps in the village and knew how they represented the land, but didn't show the real details. Then, the answer came to him.

"It's *a map*," Tansi said confidently. "A map shows cities, forests, and rivers, but it doesn't have actual houses, trees, or water."

Wabigoon nodded approvingly. "Correct, young beaver. You are off to a good start. The second riddle awaits."

With a slow, deliberate breath, Wabigoon spoke the next riddle:

"The more of this there is, the less you see. What is it?"

Tansi thought for a moment. He had been in the deep forest many times, where the light was dim, and it was hard to see. He quickly realized the answer.

"It's *fog*," Tansi said. "The more fog there is, the less you can see because it clouds your vision."

Wabigoon smiled, his eyes twinkling. "You are indeed a clever, young beaver. But the final riddle will test your wisdom."

The wind grew still as Wabigoon spoke the last riddle:

"What is so fragile that saying its name breaks it?"

Tansi puzzled over the riddle for a long time. He thought about the things he had encountered in nature, but none seemed to fit. Then, in the quiet of the snowy mountain peak, the answer finally came to him.

"It's *silence*," Tansi said. "Silence is so fragile that even speaking breaks it."

Wabigoon's face lit up with pride. "Well done, young beaver. You have answered all three riddles correctly. The Northern Lights have shared their wisdom with you."

As the last riddle faded into the night air, the Northern Lights shimmered brighter than ever, filling the sky with their magic. Tansi felt a surge of understanding and clarity. He realized that wisdom wasn't just about being clever or fast—it was about balance, patience, and knowing when to act and when to wait. The wisdom of the Northern Lights had taught him that everything in nature was connected, and every action had its consequences. Only with understanding and respect for all things could one truly find harmony in life.

As Tansi made his way back to the village, he shared the wisdom he had gained with all the animals. He taught them that silence was important for reflection, that the more you take, the less you leave behind, and that seeing the world clearly required patience and understanding. The village flourished, and Tansi became known not only for his skills as a builder but for his deep wisdom and compassion.

Moral of The Story

True wisdom is not just about cleverness—it's about understanding the world and living in harmony with it. Wisdom requires patience, reflection, and the ability to find balance in all things.

Riddles *

❖ *"I have cities but no houses. I have forests but no trees. I have rivers but no water. What am I?"*

❖ *"The more of this there is, the less you see. What is it?"*

❖ *"What is so fragile that saying its name breaks it?"*

*Find the answer to the riddle in the back of the book.

The Snow Fox and The Spirit
of The Aurora
(A Story from Italy)

In the quiet, frozen village of *Kikik*, there lived a young snow fox named *Kaya*. Kaya was known for her quick movements, her beautiful white fur that blended perfectly with the snow, and her keen senses. However, Kaya felt that something was missing in her life. She was fast and clever, but she longed for wisdom — not just cleverness, but true understanding of the world, of the balance between the earth, sky, and all its creatures.

One cold evening, as Kaya was hunting near the edge of the village, an old raven named *Tulik* perched on a branch above her. Tulik was known as the wisest bird in the village, his feathers dark and his eyes full of mystery. He had seen many winters, and his knowledge was sought by all the creatures of the land.

"Kaya," Tulik called to her, his voice echoing in the stillness. "You are clever and fast, but there is something more you must seek — the wisdom of the Aurora. The spirit of the Northern Lights holds the knowledge you seek, but only those who prove themselves worthy by answering the three riddles of the world can claim that wisdom."

Kaya's ears perked up, and her heart fluttered with excitement. The Northern Lights — the Aurora Borealis — were said to be the spirits of the earth, sky, and water, illuminating the night with their colors. Kaya had always marveled at their beauty, and the idea that they held wisdom made her heart race. She knew that she had to seek them out and prove herself.

With a determined heart, Kaya set off into the cold wilderness. She traveled across frozen rivers, through snow-covered forests, and up the steep, icy slopes of the mountains. Her journey was long and difficult, but Kaya's spirit remained strong. After many days, she finally reached a high plateau where the night sky was illuminated by the shimmering lights of the Aurora. The sight was even more breathtaking than Kaya had imagined. The Northern Lights danced and swirled in brilliant shades of green, blue, and purple, casting an ethereal glow over the snowy landscape.

At the center of the glowing light stood a great ice-covered rock, and atop the rock stood Tulik, the wise raven. His dark feathers gleamed in the light, and his eyes sparkled with the knowledge of the ancient world.

"You have made it, Kaya," Tulik said, his voice low and wise. "To gain the wisdom of the Aurora, you must solve three riddles. The answers will reveal the balance of all things, and you will learn the true meaning of wisdom. But

remember, this is not a test of speed or strength —
it is a test of understanding and patience."

Kaya nodded, her heart filled with determination.
"I am ready, Tulik. Please, ask the riddles."

Tulik spread his wings and spoke the first riddle:

**"I have cities but no houses. I have forests but
no trees. I have rivers but no water. What am I?"**

Kaya thought hard. She had heard this riddle
before, but the answer wasn't coming easily. She
closed her eyes and remembered the maps she
had seen in the village, which showed cities,
forests, and rivers without showing any real
houses, trees, or water. The answer became clear.

"It's *a map*," Kaya said confidently. "A map
shows cities, forests, and rivers, but it doesn't
have real houses, trees, or water."

Tulik nodded approvingly. "Correct, Kaya. You
are wise indeed. But there is another riddle."

The raven's voice filled the air as he asked the second riddle:

"The more of this there is, the less you see. What is it?"

Kaya's ears twitched. She thought of the long, dark nights of winter when the snow and fog made it hard to see. The answer came to her in a flash.

"It's *fog*," Kaya said. "The more fog there is, the less you can see because it hides everything."

Tulik's eyes gleamed with approval. "Well done, Kaya. You have a sharp mind. But there is one last riddle."

With a deep breath, Tulik spoke the final riddle:

"What comes once in a minute, twice in a moment, but never in a thousand years?"

Kaya's fur bristled as she pondered the riddle. She had never heard anything like it before, and it seemed impossible to solve. She looked up at the swirling lights of the Aurora above her, and then, in the stillness of the night, the answer came to her.

"It's *the letter 'M'*," Kaya said. "The letter M comes once in a minute, twice in a moment, but never in a thousand years."

Tulik let out a soft chuckle, his eyes filled with pride. "You have answered all three riddles correctly, Kaya. You have earned the wisdom of the Aurora."

As Kaya stood beneath the shimmering lights, she felt a deep sense of understanding wash over her. The wisdom of the Aurora was not just knowledge—it was the realization that all things are connected. The land, the sky, the creatures— they all existed in harmony, and only by understanding that balance could one truly find peace and wisdom. Kaya understood now that wisdom was not about being the fastest or the cleverest, but about seeing the world with patience, respect, and understanding.

When Kaya returned to the village, she shared the lessons she had learned with all the creatures. She taught them the importance of balance in nature, of respecting the land and the sky, and of understanding that true wisdom came from within—through patience, reflection, and connection to the world around them.

Moral of The Story

True wisdom comes from understanding the balance of nature and the connections between all things. It is not about speed or cleverness, but about patience, respect, and the ability to see the world with clarity.

Riddles *

- ❖ *"I have cities but no houses. I have forests but no trees. I have rivers but no water. What am I?"*
- ❖ *"The more of this there is, the less you see. What is it?"*
- ❖ *"What comes once in a minute, twice in a moment, but never in a thousand years?"*

Find the answer to the riddle in the back of the book.

Layla and The Wisdom
of The Desert Winds
(A Story from Arabia)

In a peaceful village near the oasis, there lived a young girl named *Layla*. Layla was known for her beauty, her kindness, and her determination. The villagers loved her, but Layla had always felt there was something more she needed to understand. She often sat by the edge of the oasis, staring out at the endless desert, wondering what secrets it held. She heard the whispers of the winds, the stories that seemed to float on the air, but she could never quite grasp their meaning.

One evening, as the golden sun dipped below the horizon and the stars began to shine, an old and wise falcon named *Zayid* landed near Layla. Zayid had lived many years, traveling across the desert and learning its many secrets. He was known for his sharp eyes and even sharper mind. He looked at Layla with his wise, piercing gaze.

"Layla," Zayid said, his voice carrying over the soft desert winds, "the desert speaks to those who listen carefully. The winds carry with them the wisdom of the ages, but only those who seek the truth will hear it. There are three winds that guide the desert: the North Wind, the South Wind, and the West Wind. Each of them carries a riddle. If you can solve them, you will understand the heart of the desert, and the desert will share its wisdom with you."

Layla's heart skipped a beat. She had always wanted to understand the desert, and now it seemed like she had the chance. She asked, "How do I find these winds, Zayid?"

The falcon spread his wings and pointed toward the horizon. "The winds come at different times, and they reveal themselves only to those who are ready. You must travel to the Three Dunes — the highest dunes in the desert—where each wind will meet you and test your wisdom. If you answer the riddles, the desert will open its heart to you."

With newfound resolve, Layla set off the next morning. She journeyed across the endless sands, the heat of the sun beating down on her, but her determination kept her moving forward. After several days, she reached the first of the Three Dunes, a high peak that stood like a golden tower against the clear sky. There, a soft breeze brushed against her face—the North Wind had arrived.

The wind spoke, its voice like a whisper carried on the air:

"I can fly without wings. I can cry without eyes. Wherever I go, darkness follows me. What am I?"

Layla closed her eyes and listened to the wind. She had seen many things in her life, but this riddle felt different. Then, she thought of the storm clouds that would roll in from the north, darkening the sky and bringing rain. The answer became clear.

"It's *a cloud*," Layla said confidently. "A cloud can float without wings, it can bring rain that makes it seem like it is crying, and it brings darkness with it wherever it goes."

The North Wind swirled around her, and a soft voice echoed, "Correct, Layla. You have answered wisely, and you may now proceed to the second dune."

With that, Layla traveled to the second dune, where the air was cooler, and the sands were rippled by gentle breezes. As she climbed to the top, the South Wind, warm and comforting, met her.

The wind whispered:

"I am not alive, but I grow; I don't have lungs, but I need air; I don't have a mouth, but water kills me. What am I?"

Layla thought carefully. She had seen many things in the desert—plants, animals, and the constant cycle of life. But this was a tricky one. Then, she remembered the fires that the desert nomads would light, fires that could grow when fed by dry wood, but would be extinguished by water.

"It's *fire*," Layla said, her voice steady. "Fire grows when it has air and fuel, but it is extinguished by water."

The South Wind gently lifted the grains of sand around her and spoke, "You are wise, Layla. The desert shares its knowledge with those who understand its ways. Now, you may go to the third dune."

Layla thanked the wind and made her way to the final dune, where the evening breeze was cool and strong. As she reached the top, the West Wind, soft yet powerful, greeted her.

The West Wind spoke in a deep, calm voice:

"The more you take, the more you leave behind. What am I?"

This riddle was not as difficult, for Layla had heard it many times in the village, but it was one that she had to think about carefully. She had seen the footprints of travelers across the desert, and it clicked.

"It's *footsteps*," Layla answered with a smile. "The more steps you take, the more footprints you leave behind."

The West Wind swirled around her in a gentle dance, and the voice of the wind said, "You have answered all the riddles, Layla. You are now wise in the ways of the desert. Remember that wisdom is not just knowing the answers, but understanding the balance of life. The desert, the winds, the sand — they are all connected, and they share their secrets with those who are patient and seek truth."

As Layla made her way back to the village, she felt a deep sense of peace and understanding. She had solved the riddles of the Three Winds, and in doing so, she had gained the wisdom she had always sought. She shared her newfound knowledge with the villagers, teaching them to respect the desert's balance, to listen to the winds, and to seek wisdom in all things.

Moral of the Story

Wisdom is not just about cleverness or quick answers; it's about understanding the world around you, respecting its balance, and being patient enough to listen and learn.

Riddles *

- ❖ "I can fly without wings. I can cry without eyes. Wherever I go, darkness follows me. What am I?"

- ❖ *"I am not alive, but I grow; I don't have lungs, but I need air; I don't have a mouth, but water kills me. What am I?"*

- ❖ *"The more you take, the more you leave behind. What am I?"*

*Find the answer to the riddle in the back of the book.

The Legend of The Jaguar
and The Moonlit Mountain
(A Story from Mexico)

In a beautiful village nestled at the edge of the jungle, there lived a young jaguar named *Zoltek*. Zoltek was known for his strength, agility, and speed. His sleek fur gleamed under the sun, and his keen senses allowed him to navigate the dense jungle with ease. But despite his physical prowess, Zoltek often wondered about the deeper mysteries of the world. He heard stories from the elders about the wisdom of the moon and the secrets hidden in the mountain. He dreamed of understanding the balance of nature and the world beyond the jungle.

One night, as Zoltek was hunting by the river, a wise old owl named *Itzel* flew down from the trees and perched on a nearby branch. Itzel was the village's storyteller, and her feathers were speckled with the same silver that shimmered in the moonlight.

"Zoltek," Itzel said in a soft, yet powerful voice, "I see that you are searching for something deeper. The moon has always watched over this land, and it holds wisdom for those who are brave enough to seek it. There is a mountain called *Cerro de la Luna*, where the moonlight shines brightest. At the peak of this mountain, there are three riddles that can open your heart to the secrets of the jungle and the stars."

Zoltek's heart raced with excitement. "I will go to the Mountain of the Moon and solve these riddles. I will find the wisdom I seek," he declared.

The wise owl nodded. "Beware, young jaguar. The journey is not easy. The riddles will test your mind and your heart. But if you are true to yourself, the moon will guide you."

With determination, Zoltek began his journey the next morning. He traveled through thick forests, crossed rivers, and climbed steep hills. He followed the path that led to *Cerro de la Luna*, where the moonlight bathed the mountain in its silvery glow. As Zoltek climbed the final stretch, he felt the presence of the moon all around him, and at the peak of the mountain, he was met by a soft breeze. There, in the pale light, stood a glowing figure: the Spirit of the Moon.

The Spirit of the Moon, glowing like a star, spoke in a voice that echoed through the night:

"To gain the wisdom you seek, you must answer three riddles. Each riddle holds a piece of the universe's secret. If you answer correctly, the jungle and the sky will open their hearts to you. But be warned—only the wisest can find the answers."

Zoltek bowed respectfully. "I am ready, Spirit of the Moon. Please, ask your riddles."

The moon spirit spoke the first riddle:

"I am not alive, but I grow; I do not have eyes, but I can see; I do not have ears, but I can hear. What am I?"

Zoltek paused and thought deeply. He had lived in the jungle all his life, and he understood that nature often spoke in ways that didn't always make sense at first. He remembered the way the plants around him would grow towards the sunlight, how the jungle seemed alive even though some things were not truly alive. The answer came to him as clearly as the moon in the night sky.

"It's *a plant*," Zoltek said confidently. "A plant grows, it can sense light and sound, but it doesn't have eyes or ears."

The Spirit of the Moon smiled. "You are wise, young jaguar. But there are two riddles left."

The second riddle came, and it was carried on the wind:

"I speak without a mouth and hear without ears. I have no body, but I come alive with wind. What am I?"

Zoltek listened carefully to the wind, feeling it rush through the trees and across the open spaces of the mountain. He thought about the way the wind could carry sounds and voices, even though it had no physical form. He had heard the wind echo through the jungle, carrying whispers from one place to another.

"It's *an echo*," Zoltek answered after a moment of thought. "An echo can speak without a mouth, hear without ears, and it is brought alive by the wind."

The Spirit of the Moon glowed brighter, and the third riddle followed:

"The more of this there is, the less you see. What am I?"

Zoltek furrowed his brow. He thought about the times when the jungle would be clouded over, when the darkness would spread across the land, making it hard to see. The answer came to him slowly, like the moon rising over the horizon.

"It's *darkness*," Zoltek said. "The more darkness there is, the less you can see."

The Spirit of the Moon beamed with light, and the voice echoed with approval. "You have answered all three riddles correctly, Zoltek. You have proven yourself worthy of the wisdom of the moon."

The moonlight shimmered, and Zoltek felt a sense of understanding wash over him. He now saw the world in a new light—he understood that the balance of nature, the harmony between the jungle and the stars, was key to all life. He realized that wisdom was not just about strength or speed, but about seeing beyond what was right in front of him, understanding the deeper forces at play in the world.

As Zoltek descended from *Cerro de la Luna*, he shared his newfound wisdom with the animals and villagers. He taught them the importance of balance, of listening to the wind, and of respecting the mysteries of the natural world. From that day on, the villagers and animals of the jungle lived in greater harmony, always guided by the wisdom of the moon.

Moral of The Story

True wisdom comes from understanding the deeper connections in the world around you. It is not just about quick answers or strength, but about patience, reflection, and seeing the unseen.

Riddles *

- ❖ *"I am not alive, but I grow; I do not have eyes, but I can see; I do not have ears, but I can hear. What am I?"*

- ❖ *"I speak without a mouth and hear without ears. I have no body, but I come alive with wind. What am I?"*

- ❖ *"The more of this there is, the less you see. What am I?"*

The Song of The Coral Reef

(A Story from the Caribbean Islands)

In a small village on one of the Caribbean islands, there lived a young parrot named *Solano*. Solano was known for his brilliant, multicolored feathers, which shimmered in the sunlight like the rainbow after a storm. But while Solano was admired for his beauty, he often felt as though something was missing from his life. He was clever and loved to mimic the songs of the village, but there was something deeper calling to him — a longing to understand the ocean and its mysteries.

The elders of the village often spoke of *Caribe*, the spirit of the ocean, who sang the songs of the coral reef. It was said that those who could hear the song would be given the wisdom of the sea and its creatures. Solano had heard the song in his dreams, a soft, haunting melody that echoed in the distance, calling him toward the water.

One day, as the sun was beginning to set, Solano perched on a branch overlooking the shimmering sea. His curiosity grew stronger with each passing day, and he felt the song of the ocean pulling at his heart. He wanted to understand its meaning, to hear the melody of the reef and discover the wisdom it held.

As if by magic, a gentle breeze rustled the palm trees, and a sea turtle named *Tashira* appeared from the waves. Tashira was the oldest and wisest creature in the village, known for her slow, deliberate movements and her deep connection to the ocean. She had traveled across the seas and had seen things that no other creature could imagine. She had heard the song of the reef many times and understood its meaning.

"Solano," Tashira said in her calm voice, "I can see that your heart is restless. You wish to understand the song of the coral reef, don't you?"

Solano nodded eagerly. "Yes, Tashira. I hear it in my dreams, but I don't know what it means. Can you help me understand it?"

Tashira smiled kindly. "The song of the reef is not just a melody, but a riddle. It is a song of balance—of the ocean, the land, and the creatures that live between them. To understand it, you must first seek the wisdom of the ocean and solve the riddle of the reef. There are three clues hidden within the waters that will reveal its meaning."

With Tashira's guidance, Solano dove into the water, his wings tucked close to his body. He swam alongside the gentle sea turtles and colorful fish, his heart full of excitement and anticipation. The coral reef stretched out before him, its colors as bright as the flowers on the island. It was a magical world—one that he had never truly seen before.

The first clue came as Solano swam deeper into the reef, near a cluster of bright orange corals. A school of fish surrounded him, and one fish spoke in a voice as clear as a bell:

"I don't have a mouth, but I can speak. I don't have ears, but I can listen. I don't have eyes, but I can see. What am I?"

Solano thought for a moment. He had heard this riddle before, and the answer came to him quickly. "It's *the wind*," he said, his voice echoing through the water. "The wind can carry sounds without a mouth, can listen by moving through trees, and can see by making the leaves dance."

The fish swirled around him in approval, and the waters seemed to shimmer with light.

"You are correct," the fish said. "The wind is the voice of the reef. It connects the ocean and the sky."

The second clue came as Solano approached a large, ancient rock that jutted from the water. The rock was covered with seaweed, and the waves crashed gently against it. A playful dolphin appeared, dancing in the water, and spoke:

"I have no legs, but I can run. I have no wings, but I can fly. I have no heart, but I can love. What am I?"

Solano pondered the riddle, watching the dolphin leap and twist in the water. Then, he realized the answer. "It's *the ocean*," Solano said with a spark of excitement. "The ocean can rush like a runner, can leap like a bird, and its waves can carry love in the hearts of those who hear its song."

The dolphin clicked in delight, and the water around them sparkled.

"Wise words, Solano," the dolphin said. "The ocean is the heartbeat of the reef, ever-changing but always present."

Finally, Solano reached the deepest part of the coral reef, where the water was calm and quiet.

There, resting on a bed of sea anemones, was an old, wise octopus named Aroha. Aroha had lived in the reef for many years and was said to know the secrets of the deep. She spoke softly, her voice bubbling through the water:

"I have no body, but I have a soul. I have no hands, but I can hold. I have no voice, but I can speak. What am I?"

Solano was stumped. He had never heard a riddle like this before. He swam in circles, thinking deeply. Then, as the light from the surface flickered on the water, the answer came to him: the coral itself.

"It's *the coral reef*," Solano said, his voice filled with certainty. "The reef has no body, yet it sustains life. It has no hands, but it holds the creatures of the sea. It has no voice, but its song speaks to the hearts of all who listen."

Aroha's eyes glowed brightly. "Yes, Solano, you have found the answer. The coral reef is the heart of the ocean, the source of life and balance. It is the song of the wind, the rhythm of the ocean, and the soul of the earth. You have learned the wisdom of the reef."

Solano felt a deep sense of peace and understanding. He had solved the riddle of the coral reef, and in doing so, he had unlocked the song that connected all things—the wind, the ocean, the reef, and all the creatures of the Caribbean.

As he flew back to the village, Solano sang the song of the reef, a melody filled with love, harmony, and wisdom. The villagers gathered around to listen, and they, too, began to understand the balance of the world around them. The ocean, the land, and the sky were all one, and the song of the reef was a reminder of that eternal connection.

Moral of The Story

True wisdom comes from understanding the interconnectedness of all things. By listening to the song of nature and respecting the balance of the world, we can live in harmony with the earth, the sea, and the sky.

Riddles *

- ❖ *"I don't have a mouth, but I can speak. I don't have ears, but I can listen. I don't have eyes, but I can see. What am I?"*

- ❖ *"I have no legs, but I can run. I have no wings, but I can fly. I have no heart, but I can love. What am I?"*

- ❖ *"I have no body, but I have a soul. I have no hands, but I can hold. I have no voice, but I can speak. What am I?"*

*Find the answer to the riddle in the back of the book.

The Spirit of the Pohutukawa Tree

(A Story from New Zealand)

In a peaceful village by the sea, there lived a young girl named *Tawhirimatea*. Tawhirimatea was known for her curiosity and her love for exploring the forest that surrounded her village. Every day, she would wander through the trees, listening to the sounds of the wind, the birds, and the rustling leaves. But there was one tree that always called to her, a grand Pohutukawa tree that stood at the edge of the forest. The tree was ancient and magnificent, with its bright red flowers blooming every summer like a fiery crown. The villagers spoke often of the tree's magic and the spirit that resided within it.

One day, Tawhirimatea's grandmother, Aroha, who was a revered elder in the village, called her to sit by the fire. "Tawhirimatea," she said, "there is a secret within the Pohutukawa tree. It is said that only those who are truly wise, brave, and kind can hear its voice. The tree holds the wisdom of the spirits and the earth. But to uncover its secrets, one must solve three riddles that will be spoken by the winds themselves."

Tawhirimatea's heart filled with excitement. "I want to understand the secrets of the Pohutukawa tree, Grandma. I want to hear its wisdom."

Aroha smiled gently. "If you seek the answers, you must first listen with your heart, not just your ears. The tree has seen the rise and fall of many generations, and its riddles are not for the faint of heart. But you, my dear, may have the courage needed."

That evening, Tawhirimatea set out on her journey to the Pohutukawa tree, her heart full of determination. As she walked through the forest, the night air was cool, and the stars above twinkled brightly, lighting her path. When she reached the tree, she sat quietly beneath its vast canopy, letting the silence envelop her.

As the wind began to stir, a soft voice spoke from the branches of the tree:

"I am not alive, yet I grow. I have no heart, but I can feel it. I have no voice, but I can sing. What am I?"

Tawhirimatea thought carefully. She had heard the elders speak of the spirit of the tree and how it was connected to the natural world. She remembered the way the tree's branches stretched wide, its flowers blooming every year, and how the birds seemed to sing as if they were speaking to the tree itself.

"The answer is *the wind*," Tawhirimatea said softly. "The wind grows as it moves, it can stir feelings in our hearts, and it carries the songs of the forest. It has no voice of its own, but it lets the world sing."

The tree's branches rustled with approval, and Tawhirimatea felt a warmth in the air as if the spirit of the tree was pleased with her answer. Then, the wind spoke again, carrying the next riddle:

"I am always with you, yet I can never be touched. I can be seen, but not held. I can travel far, but I have no legs. What am I?"

Tawhirimatea closed her eyes, listening carefully to the wind that swirled around her. She thought about the things that were always present but intangible. Then, it came to her. "It's *light*," she said with confidence. "Light is always with us, from the stars above to the fire at home. It can be seen but never touched, and it can travel across great distances without moving."

The Pohutukawa tree sighed gently, and the wind whispered with approval. The branches swayed, and the red flowers seemed to glow brighter in the moonlight.

Finally, the wind spoke one last time:

"The more I take, the more I leave behind. I am never still, and I never stop. What am I?"

Tawhirimatea thought long and hard, but this riddle felt different. She stood up, feeling the wind brush her face, and watched the stars twinkle above. As she looked at the shadows cast by the trees, the answer finally became clear. "It's *footsteps*," she said, smiling. "The more steps we take, the more footprints we leave behind. Footsteps are always moving, but they never stop, and they tell the story of where we've been."

The Pohutukawa tree creaked and swayed as the wind roared in delight. Tawhirimatea felt a rush of understanding, as if the spirit of the tree had opened her heart to the wisdom of the world.

"You have answered the riddles, Tawhirimatea," the wind whispered. "You have listened with your heart and learned the secrets of the Pohutukawa tree. The wisdom of the earth, the sky, and the spirit world is now yours to carry. Remember, the true knowledge of the world lies in balance, kindness, and understanding. You are part of this world, and the world is part of you."

As Tawhirimatea made her way back to the village, the first rays of dawn broke over the horizon, painting the sky in shades of gold and pink. She felt the spirit of the Pohutukawa tree with her, as if it had become a part of her soul. She knew that she had learned the greatest lesson of all—that wisdom and strength come not from being the loudest or the fastest, but from understanding the deeper connections that bind all living things together.

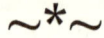

Moral of The Story

True wisdom comes from understanding the balance between all things — nature, the elements, and each other. It's not about power or speed, but about kindness, patience, and seeing the interconnectedness of life.

Riddles *

- ❖ *"I am not alive, yet I grow. I have no heart, but I can feel it. I have no voice, but I can sing. What am I?"*
- ❖ *"I am always with you, yet I can never be touched. I can be seen, but not held. I can travel far, but I have no legs. What am I?"*
- ❖ *"The more I take, the more I leave behind. I am never still, and I never stop. What am I?"*

*Find the answer to the riddle in the back of the book.

The Wise Fox
and The Riddleof The Nile
(A Story from Egypt)

Long ago, in the heart of ancient Egypt, there was a clever fox named Raheem. Raheem was known throughout the land for his sharp wit and clever tricks. He lived near the banks of the Nile River, where he often sat on the warm stones by the water, thinking of new ways to outsmart the other animals.

One bright morning, as Raheem wandered along the river, he overheard a conversation between two curious travelers, an old man and his young granddaughter. They were talking about a great treasure hidden somewhere in Egypt. The treasure, they said, could only be found by solving a very tricky riddle posed by the great goddess Hathor herself.

Intrigued by the idea of treasure, Raheem couldn't resist. He approached the travelers and, with a sly smile, asked, "I overheard your conversation. Tell me more about this riddle. If there's treasure to be found, I'd like to help you find it!"

The old man, seeing the clever fox, nodded and said, "We are trying to solve the riddle of Hathor, the goddess of wisdom. She lives deep in the desert and has guarded the treasure for centuries. To reach her, we must first solve her riddle."

The old man then recited the riddle:

"I am always hungry, I must always be fed. The finger I touch will soon turn red. What am I?"

Raheem thought deeply. He walked around the travelers, his tail flicking back and forth. "Hmm, this is a tricky one," he said, scratching his chin. "But a clever fox never gives up!"

Raheem closed his eyes and remembered the many days he spent by the river, watching the flickering flames of campfires. He thought of the warm, crackling fires that lit the night sky. He thought of how they always needed wood to burn, and how they never stopped hungry for more fuel. He smiled wide, knowing he had found the answer.

"I have the solution!" Raheem declared confidently. "The answer is fire! Fire is always hungry, and it must always be fed with wood or fuel. And the finger you touch will get burned, turning red!"

The old man and his granddaughter looked amazed. "You are right, clever fox!" they exclaimed. "We are one step closer to the treasure. We now must journey to the temple of Hathor, where the treasure lies."

They followed Raheem through the desert, where they encountered many challenges. But Raheem, with his clever mind and sharp instincts, helped them through every obstacle, from tricky sandstorms to navigating the endless dunes.

Finally, they reached the temple of Hathor, an ancient and magnificent structure covered in golden carvings. The goddess herself appeared before them, her eyes sparkling with wisdom.

"Raheem, you have solved my riddle. But remember, the greatest treasure is not gold or jewels. It is the wisdom you carry with you, the cleverness you use to help others, and the kindness you show along your journey."

Raheem smiled and bowed. He realized that the true treasure was not the gold hidden within the temple, but the knowledge he had gained and the friends he had made along the way.

Moral of The Story

The true treasure in life is wisdom, kindness, and the ability to help others. Cleverness is a gift, but it's even more valuable when used for good.

Riddle *

❖ *"I am always hungry, I must always be fed. The finger I touch will soon turn red. What am I?"*

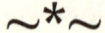

Find the answer to the riddle in the back of the book.

The Wise Yak and The Clever Rabbit
(A Story from Tibet)

Long ago, in the peaceful mountain villages of Tibet, lived a wise old yak named Tenzin. Tenzin was known far and wide for his strength, but more importantly, for his wisdom. He had lived in the mountains all his life and had seen many things. The people of the village would come to him with their questions, and he would always offer guidance.

One day, as Tenzin was grazing near the edge of the forest, a young rabbit named Lhamo hopped up to him. Lhamo was clever but not as wise as Tenzin, and he had heard many stories of the yak's great knowledge.

"Good morning, Tenzin," said Lhamo. "I have a riddle for you, and if you solve it, I will grant you a prize."

Tenzin chuckled and nodded. He loved riddles, and this was a chance for some fun.

"Very well, Lhamo. What is your riddle?"

Lhamo twitched his nose and said:

"I can be cracked, I can be made, I can be told, I can be played. What am I?"

Tenzin thought for a moment, his eyes sparkling with curiosity. He paced around slowly, as his mind worked like the wind blowing through the trees. Then, after a few moments, his deep voice echoed, "A joke! The answer is a joke!"

Lhamo's eyes widened in surprise. "That's correct! You have solved my riddle."

"But," the yak added, "I have a riddle for you as well, young rabbit. If you answer mine, I will give you a reward."

Lhamo's ears perked up with excitement. "I'm ready, Tenzin! What is your riddle?"

Tenzin looked at Lhamo with a smile and said:

"I am always with you, but you can never see me. I speak when you speak, but I have no voice of my own. I can be a friend, but I am not alive. What am I?"

Lhamo furrowed his brow. He sat down, twitching his whiskers in thought. He thought about the yak's words carefully, looking up at the sky, the mountains, and the stars. Then, after a while, his eyes lit up.

"The answer is... *your shadow!*" Lhamo exclaimed.

Tenzin nodded. "That is correct, Lhamo. Your shadow is always with you, just as wisdom is always with a true heart."

Impressed by Lhamo's cleverness, Tenzin smiled warmly. "You have earned my respect, young rabbit. I will share with you something I learned from my travels long ago."

He paused and looked down at the ground before continuing, "The lesson is this: It is not enough to be clever. One must also be wise. Wisdom teaches us to listen, to learn from each day, and to help others without expecting anything in return. You see, the greatest prize is not a gift we can hold, but the lessons we learn along the way."

Lhamo nodded, realizing the truth in Tenzin's words. From that day forward, Lhamo became known as the wise rabbit of the forest, and he shared his newfound wisdom with others in the village.

Moral of The Story

Cleverness is valuable, but true wisdom lies in listening, learning, and sharing with others.

Riddles *

- ❖ *"I can be cracked, I can be made, I can be told, I can be played. What am?"*
- ❖ *"I am always with you, but you can never see me. I speak when you speak, but I have no voice of my own. I can be a friend, but I am not alive. What am I?"*

Find the answer to the riddle in the back of the book.

The Golden Olive
and The Proud Rooster
(A Story from Greece)

In a quiet village in ancient Greece, there lived a proud rooster named Apollo. Apollo was well-known throughout the village for his beautiful, colorful feathers and his loud, confident crow that greeted the dawn each morning. He prided himself on being the first to announce the arrival of the sun, and everyone in the village admired him for his punctuality and strength.

One day, as Apollo strutted around the village square, he noticed an old man sitting beneath a large olive tree. The man was dressed in simple clothes, and beside him was a golden olive, shimmering in the sunlight.

Intrigued, Apollo strutted over to the old man and asked, "What is this golden olive? It seems to glow with great power."

The old man smiled kindly, his eyes twinkling. "Ah, young rooster, this is the Golden Olive. It is said to bring wisdom to those who possess it. But there is a condition. Only someone who can solve my riddle may take it."

Apollo puffed out his chest, confident in his intelligence and quick thinking. "I love riddles! Tell me your riddle, and I shall solve it," he declared.

The old man nodded and, with a gentle smile, spoke:

"I have keys but open no doors,
I have space but no room,
I have a face but no eyes,
I have a heart that doesn't beat.
What am I?"

Apollo was taken aback. He had solved many riddles in his time, but this one stumped him. He thought for a moment, scratching his head with his wing. He pecked at the ground and tried to focus, but the answer refused to come.

After a long silence, Apollo finally said, "I do not know the answer, wise man. Please, tell me what it is."

The old man chuckled softly. "The answer is a *piano*. A piano has keys but opens no doors, has space between its keys but no rooms, has a face but no eyes, and a heart that produces music but doesn't beat."

Apollo lowered his head, feeling embarrassed. He had never failed at a riddle before. The old man, seeing his disappointment, placed a hand gently on Apollo's wing.

"Do not be upset, my friend," he said kindly. "It is not important to know all the answers, but to seek knowledge with a humble heart. You see, the Golden Olive is not just a prize; it is a reminder that wisdom comes not only from solving riddles but from understanding that there is always more to learn."

Apollo blinked, realizing the truth in the old man's words. "So, the Golden Olive is not the greatest treasure?"

The old man smiled. "No, Apollo. The greatest treasure is the ability to seek knowledge and to share it with others. Only by remaining humble and curious can we grow wiser each day."

With that, the old man handed Apollo the Golden Olive. "Take it, young rooster, as a symbol of your journey toward wisdom. Remember, the true gift is the quest for knowledge itself."

From that day on, Apollo was no longer just the rooster who crowed at dawn. He became known throughout the village as the rooster who shared wisdom, telling tales of the importance of humility, learning, and asking questions.

Moral of The Story

True wisdom lies not in knowing all the answers but in the pursuit of knowledge and the humility to keep learning.

Riddle *

❖ *"I have keys but open no doors,*
   I have space but no room,
   I have a face but no eyes,
   I have a heart that doesn't beat.
   What am I?"

*Find the answer to the riddle in the back of the book.

The Secret of the Olive Tree
(A Story from Spain)

Long ago, in the heart of Spain, there was a young boy named Luis who lived in a village surrounded by olive groves. His family owned an old olive tree, one that was said to have been planted by his great-grandfather many years ago. It stood in the middle of the grove, its gnarled roots deep in the earth and its branches stretching toward the sky like ancient arms.

Every year, Luis's family would harvest the olives, but no one ever really talked about the tree, except for his grandmother. She always spoke of it in a special way, as if the tree held a secret.

One day, while Luis was sitting under the olive tree, playing with a few pebbles, his grandmother approached him with a twinkle in her eye.

"Luis," she said, "I see you've come to visit the tree again. Do you know what makes this tree so special?"

Luis looked up at her and shook his head. "No, Abuela. Everyone talks about this tree, but no one tells me why it's so important."

His grandmother smiled and sat down next to him. "This tree holds a secret, Luis. But to discover it, you must first solve a riddle."

Luis's eyes grew wide with excitement. He loved riddles! "A riddle, Abuela? I'm ready!"

His grandmother chuckled and said, "Here's the riddle:"

"I can be cracked, I can be made,
I can be told, I can be played.
What am I?"

Luis thought for a moment, scratching his head. The answer seemed to be just out of reach, but he refused to give up. He walked around the tree, examining its leaves and twisting branches, as if the tree itself could offer him a clue. After a while, he returned to his grandmother and said, "I don't know the answer, Abuela. Can you tell me?"

His grandmother laughed softly and said, "The answer is a *joke*, Luis. The riddle is about how a joke can be told, made, cracked, and played with. And now, let me tell you the secret of this tree."

Luis leaned forward, eager to learn. "What is it, Abuela?"

His grandmother's voice became soft and serious. "This tree is not just an olive tree. It is a symbol of the life we lead here in Spain. Like the olives that grow on its branches, we must sometimes face hardship to grow strong. We must be patient, and we must work together, just as the olives ripen slowly under the warm sun."

Luis listened carefully as his grandmother continued. "The secret of this tree is that it teaches us perseverance. It teaches us that even when we face challenges, we can turn them into something beautiful, like the olives that are made into oil. That's why this tree has been passed down for generations."

Luis thought about her words for a long time. He realized that, just like the tree, he too would face challenges in life, but that he could grow stronger by being patient and determined.

Suddenly, his grandmother's face brightened. "But there's one more thing I'll share with you, Luis. The tree also teaches us how important it is to laugh, even when things are tough. A good laugh is like the sun that helps the olives ripen. It makes everything better."

Luis smiled, understanding now. "So, the tree is a symbol of strength, patience, and laughter?"

His grandmother nodded. "Exactly, my boy. And now, the tree's secret is yours to carry with you."

Moral of The Story

Perseverance, patience, and laughter are the keys to overcoming life's challenges. Just like an olive tree that takes time to grow, we too can grow stronger through hard work and a positive attitude.

Riddle *

❖ *"I can be cracked, I can be made,*
I can be told, I can be played.
What am I?"

*Find the answer to the riddle in the back of the book.

The Clever Kangaroo
and The Great Boomerang
(A Story from Australia)

In the Australian outback, there was a clever kangaroo named Kiera. Kiera was not only known for her impressive jumping skills, but also for her sharp mind. She loved solving riddles, and her curiosity often led her on grand adventures across the wide, open plains.

One day, while hopping through the outback with her best friend, a wise old wombat named Wally, Kiera heard a commotion in the distance. She bounded over to see what was going on and found a large group of animals gathered around an old, weathered Aboriginal elder. The elder was holding a beautiful boomerang in his hands, decorated with intricate patterns.

"Ah, Kiera, Wally," the elder said with a warm smile. "It's good to see you here. I have a riddle for you, one that has been passed down through the generations. If you solve it, you'll earn the greatest reward of all—wisdom, and a special gift."

Kiera's ears perked up. She loved riddles, and the thought of earning wisdom was exciting. "What's the riddle, wise one?" she asked eagerly.

The elder raised his hands and spoke slowly:

"I fly without wings.
I cry without eyes.
Wherever I go, darkness flies.
What am I?"

Kiera thought hard. She stared at the blue sky, the distant hills, and the dry earth beneath her feet. "I know this!" she said suddenly. "The answer is *a cloud*!"

The elder nodded approvingly. "You are clever, Kiera! But there is more to this story."

He gestured toward the boomerang. "This boomerang is not just a tool for hunting or sport. It's a symbol of how life works in balance. Just as a boomerang returns to its thrower, life's actions often come back to us, for better or worse. The secret of wisdom lies in understanding that every choice you make sends something out into the world, and that same energy will always return to you."

Kiera's eyes shone with understanding. "So, the boomerang reminds us that our actions come back to us, like the way the cloud brings rain after it's flown across the sky?"

"Exactly," said the elder. "Everything we do has an effect, just as the boomerang always returns to where it started. Be mindful of your actions, for they will find their way back to you, like the clouds bringing rain to nourish the earth."

Wally, the wombat, nodded thoughtfully. "So, if we spread kindness, kindness will return to us?"

"Precisely," the elder replied. "And if we spread anger or harm, those things will also return. This is the balance we must always keep in mind."

As a reward for solving the riddle, the elder handed Kiera the beautiful boomerang. "Use it wisely, Kiera. And always remember the lessons of the clouds and the boomerang."

Moral of The Story

Every action we take has consequences, and like a boomerang, what we send out into the world will eventually come back to us. Be mindful and kind, for that is the path to wisdom and happiness.

Riddle *

❖ *"I fly without wings.*
   I cry without eyes.
   Wherever I go, darkness flies.
   What am I?"

*Find the answer to the riddle in the back of the book.

The Little Windmill
and the Great Puzzle
(A Story from Holland)

In a small village in Holland, there stood a tiny windmill that was much smaller than the grand windmills that dotted the countryside. This windmill was known as *Lucht*, which meant "wind" in Dutch. Lucht was not a grand windmill, but it was special. It was quick and nimble, turning gracefully even when the wind was light. While the larger windmills could grind the heavy grains and pump the water from the canals, Lucht had a unique gift: it could solve any puzzle!

The villagers loved Lucht and often brought it their riddles and puzzles. The windmill's blades would turn faster whenever it was thinking, as if the wind inside its wooden gears was carrying the answers. One sunny afternoon, a traveling merchant named Johan arrived in the village, carrying a large sack of beautiful wooden carvings and trinkets. As soon as he saw the little windmill, he decided to test its cleverness.

"I have heard of the little windmill who can solve any puzzle," Johan said to the villagers. "I challenge it to solve my riddle. If it can, I will leave behind my best wooden carving as a gift."

The villagers were excited to see if Lucht could solve Johan's riddle. They gathered around the small windmill, eager to watch. Lucht's blades turned gently in the breeze, waiting for the challenge.

Johan stood before the windmill, holding his chin thoughtfully. "Here is my riddle," he announced:

"What has keys but can't open locks?
What has space but no room?
What can you enter, but never leave?"

The villagers stared at each other in confusion. They didn't know the answer, and the little windmill's blades began to turn faster as Lucht thought. The windmill's wooden gears creaked and clicked as it searched for the answer.

After a few moments, Lucht's blades began to spin even faster, and with a gentle whoosh, it seemed to "speak." The answer was clear! "The answer is *a keyboard*!" Lucht seemed to say.

Johan smiled, impressed. "You are correct! A keyboard has keys but can't open locks, it has a space bar but no actual room, and you can enter it but never leave it. You have solved my riddle!"

The villagers cheered, and Johan handed over a beautiful wooden carving of a windmill as a gift. "You've earned this little windmill. I've never met such a clever windmill before."

But Johan wasn't finished. He paused for a moment and then added, "I have one more riddle, for the villagers who are gathered here today. If you can solve it, I will leave behind something even more valuable than a carving."

The villagers leaned in, eager to hear the second riddle.

Johan smiled and said:

"The more you take, the more you leave behind.
What am I?"

The villagers whispered among themselves. This time, they had an answer, thanks to Lucht. The little windmill's blades spun again, and one of the villagers, a young boy named Bram, stood up and said proudly, "The answer is *footsteps!*"

Johan laughed heartily. "That's right! The more footsteps you take, the more you leave behind. You have all earned my gratitude."

As a final gift, Johan gave the village a large, golden coin to help them with whatever they needed.

Moral of The Story

Every puzzle has a solution, and the key is to think creatively. Whether through clever thinking or working together, solutions are often closer than we realize.

Riddles *

- ❖ *"What has keys but can't open locks? What has space but no room? What can you enter, but never leave?"*
- ❖ *"The more you take, the more you leave behind. What am I?"*

*Find the answer to the riddle in the back of the book.

The Clever Crow and The Hidden River
(A Story from Bangladesh)

In a quiet village in Bangladesh, there lived a clever crow named Kalu. Kalu wasn't just any crow; he was known for his quick thinking and problem-solving skills. He loved to explore the forests, watch the farmers work, and listen to the elders tell stories of ancient times.

One hot afternoon, while Kalu was flying over the village, he overheard some villagers talking near the riverbank.

"The river has dried up!" one farmer said, shaking his head. "We've searched everywhere for the source of the river, but we can't find it. Without the river, our crops will wither."

"Who will find the hidden river?" another farmer asked. "It seems to have disappeared without a trace."

Kalu, who had always been curious, decided that he would solve this mystery. He flapped his wings and flew to the village elder's house. The wise old man, known for his knowledge of nature, often shared riddles with the children of the village.

"Elder, I overheard the villagers talking about the river that has dried up," Kalu said. "I want to help find it. Will you give me a riddle to solve, so I can discover where the river has gone?"

The elder smiled, pleased by the crow's determination. "I will give you a riddle, Kalu. Solve it, and you will find your answer."

The elder's eyes twinkled as he spoke:

"I am not alive, but I grow.
I don't have eyes, but I can see.
I don't have feet, but I can run.
What am I?"

Kalu thought for a moment, his wings slightly fluttering as he pondered the riddle. He paced back and forth, looking at the river, the fields, and the trees. After a while, his sharp eyes lit up.

"I know the answer!" Kalu exclaimed. "The answer is *the wind*!"

The elder nodded. "Correct, Kalu. The wind is not alive, but it grows stronger. It has no eyes, yet it can see the world by touching everything. It has no feet, but it can run across the land. The wind has carried the river away, but it has not disappeared entirely."

Kalu was puzzled. "What do you mean, Elder?"

The elder explained, "The wind has been strong lately, and it has caused the river to change its course. The river still flows, but in a hidden path through the mountains. To find the river, you must follow the wind."

Determined, Kalu thanked the elder and set off toward the mountains. He flew high in the sky, following the direction of the wind, feeling the breeze guiding him. After a long flight, Kalu finally spotted a narrow valley, where the wind was strongest. There, hidden behind a large rock, he found the river flowing through a secret path. The river was clear and sparkling, winding its way through the valley like a hidden treasure.

Kalu flew back to the village and shared his discovery with the farmers. The villagers cheered in delight as they followed Kalu to the hidden river, and soon, their crops began to flourish again. The village was saved, and everyone praised Kalu for his cleverness and courage.

Moral of The Story

The answer to a problem is often right in front of you, and sometimes the key to solving it is paying attention to the subtle clues around you. Curiosity and perseverance can lead to great discoveries.

Riddle *

❖ *"I am not alive, but I grow.*
I don't have eyes, but I can see.
I don't have feet, but I can run.
What am I?"

Find the answer to the riddle in the back of the book.

The Clever Snake
and The River's Secret
(A Story from Sierra Leone)

In a peaceful village near the River Rokel in Sierra Leone, there lived a wise old snake named Sewa. Sewa was not only known for his agility and strength, but also for his sharp mind. He had slithered through many lands, learning much along the way, and was greatly respected by the animals in the village. Whenever there was a problem, the animals would seek his advice.

One day, a group of animals gathered near the river. They were troubled because the river had been acting strangely. For many days, the river's flow had slowed down, and its water was becoming muddied. The fish in the river were struggling, and the villagers were worried that there would not be enough water for their crops.

The animals were all worried, but no one could figure out the cause of the problem.

Among them was a boastful lion named Baako. Baako was known for his strength and pride, and he believed that no problem was too big for him to solve. "The river has always obeyed the creatures of this land," Baako said, puffing out his chest. "I will find the source of this problem and fix it myself!"

The animals looked at Baako with skepticism, but no one dared challenge him. Instead, they turned to Sewa the snake, hoping that his wisdom could help.

"Sewa, we have heard stories of your great wisdom," said a rabbit, bowing respectfully. "Please, help us understand what is happening to the river."

Sewa, the snake, raised his head with a thoughtful glimmer in his eyes. "I will help, but first, you must answer this riddle," he said in his calm, measured voice. The animals were intrigued. Sewa had a reputation for solving problems with riddles, and they were eager to prove their cleverness.

"What has a head, a tail, but no body?"

The animals stared at one another, confused. Even Baako, the lion, looked puzzled. The rabbit twitched its ears, thinking hard. The elephant rubbed its trunk, and the monkey scratched its head. But no one could figure it out.

Sewa smiled, his tongue flicking out in amusement. "Think carefully. The answer will help you uncover the mystery of the river."

The animals were stumped for a while, but then Nia the elephant's eyes lit up. "I think I know! The answer is *a coin*," she said.

Sewa nodded with approval. "That is correct, Nia. A coin has a head and a tail but no body. Just like the river has many parts, but sometimes its true cause is hidden."

The animals were curious. "What does this riddle have to do with the river?" Baako asked, eager to know the solution.

Sewa looked thoughtfully toward the river. "The answer to the riddle lies in the flow of the river. Just as a coin can be tossed and change direction in the air, the river's flow can be disturbed. But the cause of the river's problem is not the water itself. It is the clouds that block the sun and keep the river's path cloudy and slow."

Baako, although proud of his strength, now realized that Sewa's wisdom was the key. Sometimes, the answer was not about strength but about understanding the world and its patterns.

The animals decided to follow Sewa's advice and waited patiently. Soon enough, the clouds parted, and the sun shone brightly over the river. The water began to flow freely again, and the villagers' crops were saved. The fish swam happily, and the air felt fresh and clear.

Baako, humbled by Sewa's wisdom, approached the snake. "You were right, Sewa. It was not my strength that was needed, but your wisdom. I have learned that sometimes the answers to our problems are not about brute force but about understanding nature and patience."

Sewa smiled, his tongue flicking in and out. "Remember, Baako, true strength lies in knowing when to wait and when to act. The world is full of answers, and all you need to do is look carefully."

Moral of The Story

Wisdom and patience are often more powerful than strength. Sometimes, the answers to our problems come from understanding the world around us and waiting for the right moment to act.

Riddle *

❖ *"What has a head, a tail, but no body?"*

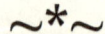

Find the answer to the riddle in the back of the book.

The Quest for The Crystal Crown

(A Story from India)

Once upon a time, in the heart of Maysoor, India, lived a curious and brave 10-year-old girl named Lila. Lila had always been drawn to magic, adventure, and mystery. Her family lived in a small village at the edge of the Enchanted Forest, where rumors of the legendary Crystal Crown had always captured her imagination. Every night, she would fall asleep dreaming of the adventures she would have when she was old enough to embark on a grand quest.

One day, the peaceful village was disrupted when a dark storm cloud appeared on the horizon, casting a shadow over the kingdom. The people were frightened, for the storm was unlike any they had seen before. It didn't rain—only dark winds howled, and the skies remained ominously black. The Queen, desperate for a solution, called upon all the wise sages and magic users of the kingdom.

A powerful wizard named Master Aria came forward. "The storm is the result of the loss of balance in the magical realms," he explained. "Only the twin of the Crystal Crown can restore harmony. The crown must be found before it's too late."

Lila's heart raced. She had heard the story of the crown before. Legends said that whoever found its twin would have the power to restore balance to the magical world.

Without hesitation, Lila stood up and declared, "I will find the twin of the Crystal Crown and restore peace to Maysoor!"

The villagers gasped. "But Lila, the journey is dangerous," they warned. "The path is filled with challenges, monsters, and traps."

Lila smiled with determination. "I've always dreamed of adventure. This is my chance to make a difference."

And so, Lila set out on her adventure, with nothing but her bravery, her sharp wit, and a magical map given to her by Master Aria. The map would guide her, but it could only reveal the next step of the journey once she had proven herself worthy of it.

The Enchanted Forest

Her first stop was the Enchanted Forest, where ancient trees whispered secrets and creatures of all kinds roamed free. As Lila ventured deeper into the forest, she came across a shimmering pond. At the edge of the pond sat a talking frog.

"Who dares enter the realm of the pond of truth?" croaked the frog. "To pass, you must answer my riddle."

Lila was excited. "I love riddles!" she said, her eyes sparkling.

The frog grinned and asked:

"I am not alive, but I grow. I don't have lungs, but I need air. I don't have a mouth, but water kills me. What am I?"

Lila thought hard. She looked at the pond, the trees, and the sky. Then it hit her.

"A fire!" she exclaimed.

The frog nodded in approval. "Correct! You are wise beyond your years. The path ahead is open to you."

Lila smiled and walked on, the forest now feeling even more magical. The frog had granted her the gift of insight.

The Caves of Echoing Shadows

Her next destination was the Caves of Echoing Shadows. The caves were known for their illusions, where shadows would trick travelers into walking the wrong path. Inside the caves, Lila found herself surrounded by eerie whispers and shifting shadows. But Lila wasn't fooled. She had always been clever, and the lesson of the frog still echoed in her mind: "Trust your instincts, not what you see."

Suddenly, the shadows formed into the shape of a giant serpent, hissing at her, its eyes glowing red.

"You cannot pass without facing me," it said in a booming voice. "I will give you a challenge."

Lila stood firm. "What challenge do you have for me, serpent?"

The serpent grinned and said, "I will give you a riddle. Solve it, and you may continue your journey. Fail, and you will remain here forever."

The riddle was:

"I have cities, but no houses. I have forests, but no trees. I have rivers, but no water. What am I?"

Lila pondered for a 8moment. "This one is easy," she said with confidence. "It's a map!"

The serpent's eyes widened, and it slithered back into the shadows. "You are clever, child. You have passed my test."

Lila continued deeper into the caves, her courage and intellect lighting her way.

The Mountain of Eternal Winds

Finally, after many days of travel, Lila reached the Mountain of Eternal Winds, where the twin of the Crystal Crown was said to be hidden. The winds were so strong here that they could blow away anyone unprepared. Lila, however, had learned much on her journey and was ready for this final challenge.

At the peak of the mountain, she found a pedestal with a glowing crystal crown upon it. But just as she reached out to take it, a voice echoed through the winds.

"You have done well, young one," said the voice of the wind itself. "But before you take the crown, I must ask you one last question. This question will determine if you are truly worthy of this gift."

Lila stood tall and replied, "I'm ready."

The wind's voice grew soft, almost like a whisper: **"What is the greatest treasure in the world?"**

Lila closed her eyes, feeling the wind on her face, and thought deeply. She knew the answer was not about wealth or power.

"The greatest treasure is love," she said. "Love for others, love for the world, and love for the journey we take together."

There was a moment of silence before the wind whispered, "You are truly worthy, Lila."

With that, the crystal crown floated gently into her hands, glowing with a soft, radiant light.

The Return Home

Lila returned to the kingdom of Maysoor, the twin crown in her hands. As soon as she placed it next to the Queen's crown, a surge of magic spread throughout the kingdom, calming the storm and restoring balance to the land.

The villagers cheered, and the Queen smiled warmly at Lila. "You have proven that the greatest strength is not in how far you can go, but in how much love and wisdom you share along the way."

Lila smiled back, knowing that her journey was just beginning. She had learned that true magic wasn't about finding treasures, but about finding kindness, courage, and wisdom within yourself and sharing them with the world.

Moral of The Story

True adventure is 8not about the destination, but about the journey and the lessons you learn along the way. Love, wisdom, and kindness are the greatest treasures you can share with others.

Riddles *

- ❖ *"I am not alive, but I grow. I don't have lungs, but I need air. I don't have a mouth, but water kills me. What am I?"*
- ❖ *"I have cities, but no houses. I have forests, but no trees. I have rivers, but no water. What am I?*

Find the answer to the riddle in the back of the book.

Answers to Riddles

1. The Silver Snow Fox and The Star

❖ "I have no voice, but I can speak to you. I have no body, but I can be touched. What am I?"

Answer: A thought.

❖ "I can travel the world, but I stay in one place. I can be seen but never touched. I light the sky, but never burn. What am I?"

Answer: A star.

2. The Wise Sparrow and The Golden Pomegranate

❖ "I have cities, but no houses. I have forests, but no trees. I have rivers, but no water. What am I?"

Answer: A map.

❖ "I am tall when I am young and short when I am old. What am I?"

Answer: A candle.

❖ "What was the most precious gift?"

Answer: The most precious gift is kindness.

3. The Brave Turtle and The Rainbow Stone

❖ "I am not alive, but I grow; I do not have lungs, but I need air; I do not have a mouth, but water kills me. What am I?"

Answer: *Fire.*

❖ "I can be cracked, made, told, and played. What am I?"

Answer: *A joke.*

4. The Brave Highland Deer and The Stone of The Lost

❖ "I speak without a mouth and hear without ears. I have no body, but I come alive with the wind. What am I?"

Answer: *An echo.*

❖ "The more of this there is, the less you see. What am I?"

Answer: *Darkness.*

5. The Mountain Fox and The Heart of The Northern Lights

❖ "I have keys but open no doors. I have space but no room. I have a face but no features. What am I?"

Answer: *A keyboard.*

❖ "I can be cracked, I can be made, I can be told, I can be played. What am I?"

Answer: A joke.

6. The Clever Crane and The Jade Emperor's Secret

❖ "I speak without a mouth and hear without ears. I have no body, but I come alive with the wind. What am I?"

Answer: An echo.

❖ "The more you take, the more you leave behind. What am I?"

Answer: Footsteps.

7. The Lion and The Golden Horn

❖ "I can fill a room, but I take up no space. What am I?"

Answer: Light.

❖ "I am always hungry; I must always be fed. The finger I touch, will soon turn red. What am I?"

Answer: Fire.

❖ "The more you take, the more you leave behind. What am I?"

Answer: Footsteps.

8. The Jaguar and The Spirit of The Amazon

❖ "I have cities, but no houses. I have forests, but no trees. I have rivers, but no water. What am I?"
Answer: A map.

❖ "I am always in front of you, but you can never see me. I am the key to your future, yet I am always hidden. What am I?"
Answer: The future.

❖ "The more you take, the more you leave behind. What am I?"
Answer: Footsteps.

9. The Crane and The Hidden Pond

❖ "The more you take, the more you leave behind. What am I?"
Answer: Footsteps.

❖ "I have keys but open no doors. I have space but no room. You can enter, but you can't go outside. What am I?"

Answer: A piano.

10. The Coconut and The Wise Owl

❖ "The more you take, the more you leave behind. What am I?"

Answer: Footsteps.

❖ "I have keys but open no doors. I have space but no room. You can enter, but you can't go outside. What am I?"

Answer: A piano.

❖ "The more you have of me, the less you see. What am I?"

Answer: Darkness.

11. The Bamboo and The Clever Monkey

❖ "I am always hungry, I must always be fed. The finger I touch, will soon turn red. What am I?"

Answer: Fire.

❖ "The more you take, the more you leave behind. What am I?"

Answer: *Footsteps.*

❖ "I have keys but open no doors. I have space but no room. You can enter, but you can't go outside. What am I?"

Answer: *A piano.*

12. The Great Northern Lights and The Brave Beaver

❖ "I have cities but no houses. I have forests but no trees. I have rivers but no water. What am I?"

Answer: *A map.*

❖ "The more of this there is, the less you see. What is it?"

Answer: *Fog.*

❖ "What is so fragile that saying its name breaks it?"

Answer: *Silence*

13. The Snow Fox and The Spirit of The Aurora

❖ "I have cities but no houses. I have forests but no trees. I have rivers but no water. What am I?"

Answer: A map.

❖ "The more of this there is, the less you see. What is it?"

Answer: Fog

❖ "What comes once in a minute, twice in a moment, but never in a thousand years?"

Answer: The letter 'M'.

14. Layla and The Wisdom of The Desert Winds

❖ "I can fly without wings. I can cry without eyes. Wherever I go, darkness follows me. What am I?"

Answer: A cloud.

❖ "I am not alive, but I grow; I don't have lungs, but I need air; I don't have a mouth, but water kills me. What am I?"

Answer: Fire.

❖ "The more you take, the more you leave behind. What am I?"

Answer: Footsteps.

15. The Legend of The Jaguar and The Moonlit Mountain

❖ "I am not alive, but I grow; I do not have eyes, but I can see; I do not have ears, but I can hear. What am I?"

Answer: A plant.

❖ "I speak without a mouth and hear without ears. I have no body, but I come alive with wind. What am I?"

Answer: An echo.

❖ "The more of this there is, the less you see. What am I?"

Answer: Darkness.

16. The Song of The Coral Reef

❖ "I don't have a mouth, but I can speak. I don't have ears, but I can listen. I don't have eyes, but I can see. What am I?"

Answer: The wind.

❖ "I have no legs, but I can run. I have no wings, but I can fly. I have no heart, but I can love. What am I?"

Answer: The ocean.

❖ "I have no body, but I have a soul. I have no hands, but I can hold. I have no voice, but I can speak. What am I?"

Answer: The coral reef.

17. The Spirit of the Pohutukawa Tree

❖ "I am not alive, yet I grow. I have no heart, but I can feel it. I have no voice, but I can sing. What am I?"

Answer: The wind.

❖ "I am always with you, yet I can never be touched. I can be seen, but not held. I can travel far, but I have no legs. What am I?"

Answer: Light.

❖ "The more I take, the more I leave behind. I am never still, and I never stop. What am I?"

Answer: Footsteps

18. The Wise Fox and The Riddleof The Nile

❖ "I am always hungry, I must always be fed. The finger I touch will soon turn red. What am I?"

Answer: Fire.

19. The Wise Yak and The Clever Rabbit

❖ "I can be cracked, I can be made, I can betold, I can be played. What am?"

Answer: A joke.

❖ "I am always with you, but you can never see me. I speak when you speak, but I have no voice of my own. I can be a friend, but I am not alive. What am I?"

Answer: *Your shadow.*

20. The Golden Olive and The Proud Rooster

❖ "I have keys but open no doors,
I have space but no room,
I have a face but no eyes,
I have a heart that doesn't beat.
What am I?"

Answer: *A piano.*

21. The Secret of the Olive Tree

❖ "I can be cracked, I can be made,
I can be told, I can be played.
What am I?"

Answer: *A joke.*

The Riddle Vault

A Treasure Trove of Mind-bending Puzzles and Brain Teasers.

❖ What can you catch but not throw?
Answer: A cold!

❖ What gets dirtier the more you wash it?
Answer: Water

❖ I have teeth but do not eat. What am I?

Answer: A comb!

❖ What gets wetter the more you dry?
Answer: A towel!

❖ What is it: it falls standing up and runs lying down?
Answer: Rain!

❖ What is it: the more you take away, the bigger it gets?

Answer: A hole!

❖ What is designed for walking but never takes a step?

Answer: The street!

❖ What goes up but never comes down?

Answer: Your age!

❖ What has a face but no eyes or mouth?

Answer: A clock!

❖ What doesn't get wet even when it rains?

Answer: A shadow!

❖ I am seen by everyone, yet I have no eyes.

Answer: The mirror!

❖ It's yours, but your friends use it more than you.

Answer: Your name!

❖ What is ever-present but invisible to the eye?

Answer: Time!

❖ What is something everyone has, but no one can touch or hold?

Answer: Memory!

❖ I have a head, but I do not have a brain. I have a point, but I do not feel pain. What am I?

Answer: A needle!

❖ I fall but never get hurt. I am cold but never complain. What am I?
Answer: Snow!

❖ I have four legs but I can't walk? What am I?

Answer: The chair!

❖ I run, but never walk. I have a bed, but I never sleep. What am I?
Answer: A river!

❖ I rise in the morning without being called, and disappear at night without being stolen. What am I?
Answer: The sun!

❖ I am something that you can never change, no matter how much you want to. What am I?
Answer: The past!

❖ I build the future, brick by brick,

with sweat and toil, I make it stick.

Though I may tire you, don't retreat,

For in the end, the reward's sweet.

What am I?

Answer: Hard work!

❖ I take you far and wide,

With every step, I'm by your side.

No end, no start,

I'm always near, yet I move forward, year

by year. What am I?

Answer: A journey!

❖ What moves across the sun yet leaves no

shadow behind?

Answer: The wind!

❖ I'm a bird that cannot fly,

But I'm the symbol of a land where I lie.

I'm brown and I'm small, and I hop on the

ground,

What am I, always seen, but never in the

sky?

Answer: A kiwi!

❖ I grow with time, and guide your way,
   More valuable than riches, I stay. What
   am I?
   Answer: Wisdom!

❖ I roar without a voice, and flash without a
   light,
   I shake the sky, but I'm gone in a flight.
   What am I?
   Answer: Thunder!

❖ I can make you chuckle or cause a moan,
   But I'm at my best when I'm widely
   known.
   What am I?
   Answer: A joke!

❖ I'm a tree with leaves of silver and green,
   My fruit is small, yet it's quite serene.
   I've been around for ages, strong and
   wise,
   What am I, that grows under sunny
   skies?

   Answer: An olive tree!

❖ I'm made of water, but I'm not the sea,

I float in the sky, light and free.

I can bring storms or just pass by,

What am I that fills the sky?

Answer: A cloud!

❖ I flow without feet, I never stand still,

I carve through the land, against my will.

I can be calm, or rush with force,

What am I, on my endless course?

Answer: A river!

❖ I'm soft and quiet, I can't be loud,

I carry secrets, but never a crowd.

I slip through cracks, I hide with ease,

What am I, that you can barely seize?

Answer: A whisper!

❖ I roar but I have no voice,

I flash but I have no light.

I bring rain, wind, and strife,

What am I, that disrupts life?

Answer: A storm!

❖ I'm dark inside but full of treasure,

I hide secrets, beyond measure.

With walls that echo and floors that bend,

What am I, where the journey may end?

Answer: A cave!

❖ What has hands but can't clap?

Answer: A clock!

❖ What has to be broken before you can use it?

Answer: An egg!

❖ What has a neck but no head?

Answer: A bottle!

❖ I jump when I walk and sit when I stand. What am I?

Answer: A kangaroo!

❖ What is full of holes but still holds water?

Answer: A sponge!

❖ The person, who makes it, sells it.

The person who buys it never uses it.

The person who uses it never knows they're using it. What is it?

Answer: A coffin!

❖ The more you share me, the less you have. What am I?

Answer: A secret!

❖ What begins with T, ends with T, and has T in it?

Answer: A teapot!

www.ingramcontent.com/pod-product-compliance
Lightning Source LLC
Chambersburg PA
CBHW031417250626
47155CB00004B/1527